WANTED

AN ARTIST SEEKING REDEMPTION.
A WANDERER NEEDING PERMANENCE.
AND THE CRAZY THAT'LL MAKE OR BREAK THEM.

R.E. HARGRAVE

SUMMARY

An artist seeking redemption.
A wanderer needing permanence.
And the crazy that'll make or break them.

Hyde Johnson is an erotic audiobook *performer*. A 'Read By' byline is too plain, and 'Narrated By' still doesn't capture what he does. His livelihood is his passion. Performance art, the air he breathes. Which translates to a recluse who is a hot mess. He's not eating right, he's drinking more, and his family's meddling is making it harder to stay on task.

Being designated the guardian of her young niece Tina is the last thing Gypsy Hartford expected.

But when the State of South Carolina unceremoniously puts Tina in her care, Gypsy accepts it's time to grow up and stop floating from town to town. Where does she start when she has no degree, no real friends, and no family besides Tina?

A want ad could be the answer to both their conundrums. Or it might open a whole new can of worms. Especially when you throw in a crazed author with an unhealthy obsession for her narrator.

Someone to run errands, cook, and handle minor cleaning. Must be quiet and self-starting as I work nights and sleep during the day. Compensation negotiable, including transportation and board. Discretion a MUST.

Only serious inquiries please.

This one is for Trevor and Jess, without whose suggestion and encouragement I doubt I would have been inspired to write this story.

"*E*asing his tongue into her mouth was more sensation than his body could handle—"

"Unca Hyde, sissies chase me. Halp!"

The tiny voice, paired with a banging fist, called through the door of his studio, bringing Hyde's recording session to an abrupt halt.

Why his brother thought they needed a fourth kid when they had three monsters already was beyond him. Removing his headphones and switching off the mic, Hyde marked his script, saved everything, and shut down. Heavy feet dragged him to the door, which he opened to glare down into the wide eyes of Randy, his three-year-old nephew. A few seconds later, giggles drew his attention to the top of the stairs where Aimee and Ashlee, the twelve-year-old twins, stood on the right side of breaking the house rule: no one under eighteen was to step onto the upstairs landing.

They were close, but unlike their brother, they hadn't crossed the line.

Since moving back into his childhood home, he'd remodeled the second floor of the old converted schoolhouse into his recording haven and business, Hush Studios. A small kitchenette and bath were at one end; the rest soundproofed and kitted out with the best audio and technical equipment he could get his hands on. Via the internet, of course, because Hyde Johnson didn't leave his house unless he absolutely had to.

"Unca Hyde." Randy tugged his hand, and Hyde let out a ragged sigh.

Sami was going to be less than pleased. Ms. Jackson, the author he'd narrated five projects for in the last two years, had been getting more demanding of late. Entitled even. It wasn't *his* fault Zeke had shown up unannounced two weeks ago with his wife and kids and interrupted the recording of number six. Hyde's meticulous nature meant this delay was driving him mad.

Two days, he reminded himself. *They'll be gone in two more days.*

"Where's your mom and dad, kid?" Hyde directed his glare at the twins even though he was speaking to Randy.

Their faces sobered before they turned around and disappeared down the stairs.

He gave a satisfied nod and looked down at his visitor. "There ya go, Randy. They're gone. Off you go to bed now, I've got work to do."

"You always say dat, Unca Hyde." The little boy shuffled his feet and tugged harder on Hyde's hand. "Come read me story. Pwease?"

"You aren't going to take no for an answer, are you?"

Randy shook his head, and Hyde huffed.

Fuck. Why not, my concentration is already screwed, he thought. "Lead the way, kid."

An hour, and three stories, later, Hyde stood and stretched his back. Randy had put up quite the fight falling asleep. Wondering if his animated reading had kept the little tyke up, he made his way out to the hall and closed the door behind him. He turned and jumped at the sight of Zeke and

Connie leaning against the wall a few feet down, smiles on their faces.

"What?" Hyde grouched at the pair.

Zeke shook his head. "Nothing, brother."

"Everything, Hyde," overrode Connie. "It's not too late for you to settle down and be a daddy, ya know? You'd make a good one."

Hyde scoffed then trudged past them. Before he turned the corner, he looked back and snapped, "Remind your fucking kids to stay off the second floor. I'm behind schedule."

Fifteen minutes later, he had everything almost ready to resume his performance of Tristan, the warrior lover with a wicked tongue.

First things first, though. Hyde went over to the wet bar, pulled the bottle of Effen from inside and poured a two-finger shot, then slammed it. The vodka burned on the way down, leaving a crisp, clean cucumber taste in its wake.

Now he was ready.

Jesus, his head throbbed. Hyde blinked heavy lids against the artificial lighting of the studio. The broken windows had long been sealed and blacked out in the remodel. Crawling into a sitting position on the couch, he swung his gaze around the room, eyes landing on the empty vodka bottle.

So much for my one shot per session rule.

Who was he kidding? He hadn't adhered to that rule in months. He chuckled, then winced. Tylenol, coffee, and a hot shower followed by a long stint in his bed were needed. In that order.

After a quick trip down the hall to relieve himself, he ducked back into the studio office to check things over before he closed up shop for the day. A message box, the little missed notification bubble indicating the sender's eagerness with its 20+, blinked at him from the bottom of his screen. He knew who it was without checking.

Sami.

Hyde's eyes still had sleep in them and weren't focusing well, so he played the audio on the messages.

Hyde, it's Sami, just wanted to see how we were doing. Thought I was supposed to get the next five chapters today...

Sami again. Hey, I was really counting on those chapters before I went to bed. Let me know.

What the hell, Hyde? Do I not pay you enough to warrant getting my shit on time?

Her distinct northeast accent was slurring by

that point, so Hyde turned it off. He'd heard enough anyway. Recent history had proven the messages would progress to sexual aggression by the end of her tantrum. A smart man would be ending this business relationship. Yes, she paid him well, but that didn't mean she owned him. Still, instead of heading to the coffee he knew his java-addicted sibling had brewed downstairs at the crack of dawn, he spent the next hour doing a quick edit on the chapters he'd managed to record in the early hours of the morning.

Not a bad batch, all things considered, he praised himself as he uploaded the files, added a brief note of apology with a reminder of his unexpected visitors, and then marched off to find his goddamn coffee.

Coming upon the kitchen, Hyde slowed when he heard his name mentioned. Zeke and Connie's hushed voices suggested plotting. He moved as close as he dared to the doorframe, and leaned in to listen.

"It's not right, how he stays alone all the time. This is the worst we've seen him, Zeke. I swear he's lost more weight. We've got to do something to help him."

"You know how stubborn he is, Connie. I've

offered multiple times to have him move down to Charleston with us. He refuses to leave this house, though. I don't know if he expects they'll come back someday and he'll get some kind of closure, or what. With any luck, he'll eventually accept the punks got away with it, and that there's no point wasting energy on what-ifs or revenge."

Their words made him bristle. The pair of them could go fuck themselves. If he'd been home working on his acting skills, instead of at Clemson chipping away at an economics degree he would never use – but his parents had insisted he needed – he could have saved them. Hyde had always been a night owl, so had no doubts he would've been awake, and alert, on that particular night.

He wouldn't have had to be pulled out of class the next day, hundreds of miles away, because his brother had come to the campus to speak to him. To explain their mother and father had been slaughtered in their bed while they slept so some assholes could smash up the place and raid the liquor cabinet. Besides the booze, all the intruders had taken were his parents' lives.

The crime scene was discovered because their old Irish setter showed up at the neighbor's house. When Mr. Miller drove Rusty home, he'd called the police after noticing the upper windows broken and the front door standing wide open.

Hyde shook off the cold memories and strode into the kitchen. "What time are you out of here tomorrow? I'm getting the hard press from my client. Y'all have cost me hours in the studio with your impromptu visit." An undercurrent of warning laced his terse tone.

"Good morning to you, too, sunshine," Zeke deadpanned.

"Hyde, I'm sor—"

"Save it, Connie." Her back straightened when he cut her off, making her baby bump more prominent.

"Connie's looking out for you. There's no need for you to be an asshole, man."

Shrugging, Hyde poured his coffee. "Guess it comes naturally," he snarked before taking a much-needed sip of black gold. The hot liquid helped at once. "Sorry, long night," he murmured, and then looked up to face them.

Pity and concern stared back.

"Listen, Hyde, we were talking."

"I know. I heard."

Zeke half-smiled. "Yes, well, we all know you aren't leaving. I get it. This is a cool place, to be fair. I loved growing up here. Who would've thought an old school building would make such an awesome living space, right?"

Hyde grinned as a memory of a childhood round of hide-and-seek in the vast abode flashed through his head.

"Have you considered getting some help in?"

His grin fell. "What do you mean?"

"Someone to help out around here, with the domestic-y stuff. Some real food would do you good, too," Connie hedged. "I know you're a big boy and all that, Hyde, but I did have to do some tidying when we arrived. You're spending all your time upstairs, living on takeout and vodka—"

"If you don't like it, get out. I didn't invite you. And I sure as fuck didn't ask you to clean my shit."

Hyde ignored his brother's angry yelling following after him as he went to his room. He had his coffee. Next was Tylenol and a shower.

One more day to go.

CHAPTER ONE

Gypsy looked over at her sleeping niece and felt a tad jealous. She hadn't had a good night's sleep since getting the call that her sister, whose husband passed from a heart attack the year before, was dying. In the blink of an eye, while she sat by Gloria's hospital bed, her older sister succumbed to the rare Bourbon virus as the result of a tick bite—leaving an eleven-year-old in Gypsy's charge. Through age and illness, the rest of their family were already gone. With the exception of possible long lost relatives, Tina and Gypsy only had one another now. The whole situation was a mess which boggled the mind.

She barely took care of herself, what was she going to do with a kid?

The call, by coincidence, had come while Gypsy was enjoying Hilton Head Island, so she hadn't been far from her sister's posh, wooded home in upstate South Carolina. Since turning eighteen, a roaming lifestyle had carried Gypsy from city to city, letting her take time to find herself and explore the country. By finding odd jobs, most often at restaurants, or with gracious hosts, she'd passed the days and weeks of the last ten years until she either grew bored or her welcome wore out, and then she'd move on. Her possessions were few, her heart light.

Well, they had been.

Tina cried out in her sleep, and Gypsy sighed.

Poor, sweet girl.

First thing in the morning, she'd grab a local paper and check the want ads. If she could find something so they could stay in Roebuck, maybe Tina's life could be spared further unnecessary disruption. They'd put Gloria in the ground two days before, next to Jim. It'd been the first time Gypsy visited her brother-in-law's grave; she'd been out on a yacht, enjoying a small fling with a feisty Cuban from the Florida Keys when Jim's funeral was held, so had missed it.

One thing was unquestionable. There was no

way they'd be keeping Gloria's house. It was way out of Gypsy's non-existent budget.

Gypsy's eyes ached from poring over the paper in front of her. Across the table, Tina munched on her second donut. Her orange juice hadn't been touched. She pushed the glass toward her niece with a low cough and a, "You promised."

Tina rolled her eyes but grabbed the glass and emptied half of it. "Happy?"

"For now."

So far, the job opportunities in the immediate area were scarce. The few listings she'd found all wanted a degree, which she didn't have. There were no certificates issued in the school of life, after all. She hadn't looked at rentals yet, but dreaded what they were going to cost.

Overhead a bell chimed, announcing the arrival of a family of five into the diner. The father's youthful appearance was striking considering the teenaged twins standing next to him. They suggested a more advanced age. *Must be the fair hair and eyes,* she mused.

The mother caught Gypsy staring, and smiled.

Embarrassed, Gypsy dropped her head and

went back to reading the ads. A few moments later the family was being seated at the table next to her, putting them within earshot as they began talking amongst themselves. Her ears perked up at the topic.

"I don't know about all this, Connie. Posting an ad for a live-in assistant, without his knowledge or consent, can't end well."

"We could go straight to an agency and hire someone for him instead, but we have to do something before he wastes away. So, tell me, how does this sound?" There was a pause as the woman dug a notebook out of her purse and then flipped through it. Clearing her throat, she read out: "Wanted. Someone to run errands, cook, and handle minor cleaning. Must be quiet and self-starting as I work nights and sleep during the day. Compensation negotiable, including transportation and board. Discretion a *must*. Only serious inquiries please." She waved her hand around. "Just needs a phone number and an email added, and then we're ready to post, right?"

Her expression was tired, but hopeful as the father dropped his head into his hands and shook it.

A muffled, "He's gonna kill me," followed.

Impulse yanked Gypsy to her feet and led her to their table. "Um, excuse me?"

The man looked up at her in confusion, while the woman eyed her with curiosity.

"I'm sorry to bother you, but I overheard you talking, and, well, I've recently been placed in a situation with my niece," she nodded toward Tina who was gawping back at her, "and I need a job, like yesterday, that's local. Maybe we can help each other?"

The woman smiled and extended her hand. "I'm Connie Johnson, and this is my husband Zeke, why don't you and your niece join us for breakfast?"

An hour later, bellies satiated, Zeke was hugging his kids and kissing his wife while Gypsy assured Tina everything would be fine. She also promised not to make any final decisions without talking to Tina first.

"She'll be fine, Gypsy. Tina and the girls will have a blast. Come on, I'll drive."

Connie and the kids had been dropped off at a nearby roller-skating rink, to keep them busy while Zeke took Gypsy out to meet his brother Hyde.

They'd explained her potential boss was a recluse who kept to himself most of the time by working nights out of the home, and sleeping days. The Johnsons were hoping to find someone willing to help offset Hyde's reclusive ways—and keep an eye on him. The salary was negotiable because the job wasn't even a guarantee yet. Hyde still had to agree to it, and *then* he had to agree to let whoever took the position live in one of the numerous rooms and drive the car he never touched.

It sounded perfect.

It also sounded like a major crapshoot.

Gravel crunched under the tires as the minivan slowed and pulled onto a tree-lined driveway which led to a giant, red square building a quarter of a mile or so back from the road. They'd said it was an old schoolhouse, but for some reason she hadn't thought they'd been serious.

"Wow. This is awesome." Gypsy shielded her eyes to look up at the house while she climbed out of the car.

Zeke laughed. "It had its moments growing up. Let's go poke the bear." He stopped and turned to her. "Are you sure you want to do this, Gypsy? My brother can be... harsh, at times. I expect this could turn into one of those times."

"I'm willing to at least try, Mr. Johnson. I've got to for the sake of my niece. I have nowhere to go, and she shouldn't have to be uprooted from her school and friends at this time in her life."

"Okay, then. Just know there won't be any hard feelings if he goes too far and you walk out."

"You're making him out to be quite the beast." She couldn't keep the nervous giggle out of her reply.

"Let's hope the beast can be tamed," Zeke teased back then knocked on the door with his knuckles. A second later, he turned the key and pushed it open. "Welcome, Gypsy—"

"What the actual fuck, Zeke?"

They froze, and Gypsy felt her cheeks flush with heat at the sight of the angry naked man scolding at his intruders. Them.

"Oh, gosh. I'm sorry." Her hands flailed as she tried to cover her eyes.

"Jesus, Hyde! Why are you running around the house with no clothes on?"

"Fuck you. Forgive me for thinking I had the place to myself at last."

"Can you watch the language, man? There's a lady present."

"Fuck you, and fuck her. Get outta my house.

I'm about to go jerk out some pent up frustration and then sleep for twelve hours before I spend the next twelve in the booth."

Gypsy's hand dropped while she listened to the brothers go at each other. Distracted as they were, she was able to take her time with Hyde. If she'd thought Zeke was attractive at first, Hyde was superb. For a man who never got out, his physique demanded appreciation. Wavy blond hair accented piercing eyes, and those lips were such full, kissable lips...

She shook her head. If this man did become her boss, no such thing would be happening.

If? How about when?

Mr. Johnson was making it quite clear this would not be easy. Gypsy would just have to prove her usefulness. A quick glance around gave her an idea of where things might be. Head high, she strolled past the bickering men.

Hyde had been going toward a room at the end of the hall when they'd stopped him, so she went that way too, finding herself in his bedroom. A discarded robe lay across the bed. Gypsy grabbed it and went back to the living room, thrusting it in Hyde's face.

"Put this on. Have you eaten yet today?"

Blinking at her, he shook his head but took the robe.

Gypsy nodded and marched off again. Finding the kitchen this time, she threw together a bowl of ramen with mixed vegetables. The cupboard and freezer had been empty of anything else; a trip to the grocery store would be first on her agenda.

She found Hyde and Zeke at the dining room table, talking quietly. Not wanting to interrupt, she stepped over, set the soup down in front of Hyde with a smile, and then excused herself to sit in the den she'd passed in her wanderings. A few times, raised voices drifted from the other room, but for the most part their discourse seemed contained. Gypsy was on the verge of giving up that this was going to work when Zeke appeared at the doorway.

"I'm really sorry about all that. He's calmed down. Shall we start over?" he asked with a sheepish smile.

She grinned and nodded her head, then followed Zeke back to the dining room. The soup was gone, and Hyde's eyes were brighter.

"Something amusing, Miss... what was your name again?"

"Gypsy Hartford, and no, not much is amusing these days. I was just pleased to see the food helped you feel better. Just think what I can do with a stocked kitchen. Next time, I'll blow your mind."

Her chin jutted upward even as she crossed her arms, daring him to tell her she couldn't have the job. His eyes followed the movement. When they lingered on her chest, she realized her actions had lifted her boobs to make quite a display of cleavage, and she cleared her throat. Hyde's answering smirk, which revealed his dimples, made her breath catch.

Damn it all if she weren't going to have to learn to control her reactions around him.

CHAPTER TWO

yde stared at his monitor in disbelief. According to his notifications, Sami had tagged him in over a hundred Facebook posts using his twitter handle. He knew what he'd find, but had to see it for himself regardless. Sure enough, because of the tags, his name had been pulled into thousands of retweet threads. This wouldn't be a bad thing except she'd moved from labeling him her narrator or partner, to calling him her "lusty linguist lad." Like he was her personal pet or some shit. Paycheck be damned, he wasn't sure how much longer he could take this from her.

"Are you fucking kidding me?"

No one answered, of course. Hyde was alone.

Well, there was that cute little thing Zeke had

forced on him. Her tenacity had impressed, and aroused, him enough to say she could stay. If she kept out of his way. The girl had to be half his age, and therefore a piece of tail he needed to stay far, far away from. For both their sakes.

A soft ding drew his eyes to the screen, where a new message from Sami waited. He'd forgotten to make sure his status appeared unavailable and it was a tad startling how fast she'd pounced, like she'd been waiting for him to log on.

Dammit.

The blinking message box taunted him while he debated how to proceed. How far did he let this go before defending himself wouldn't cause an uproar in the Indie community and tarnish his reputation? Should he really have to point out to her that their relationship would only ever be a business partnership?

Hyde's chair squeaked as he pushed back from the antique teacher's desk. When he reached the wet bar, he was shocked to find it empty, and made a mental note to put in an order with Fernwood Liquor over in Spartanburg. Although it wasn't their norm to deliver, they delivered for him; he tipped well, and his family had been customers for decades. There was one more place to check, and he gave a low "whoop" when he found half a dozen miniature vodka bottles in the freezer of the old mini fridge he'd brought back from college. They weren't flavored, but they would do.

Cracking one open, he poured the icy contents down his throat and swallowed, thinking, *Jesus, that burns.* Pocketing two more, Hyde put the other three back in the freezer then returned to his desk. He took a deep breath, clicked on the message, and read.

Hello, big boy, how are you doing tonight?

The second mini bottle disappeared into his gut when he saw the little dots start bouncing next to her avi, indicating she'd begun typing the second she'd seen him "see" the message. This shit needed to be nipped in the bud, and pronto. Staring at her profile picture, he wondered what kind of person really lurked behind the cropped brown hair and brown eyes.

There you are! Hey! Did you see? We're

almost in the bestseller list? How exciting is that?

Hyde scoffed. The titles they'd done together had broken the top one hundred, but never the top ten; Sami liked to exaggerate. That's not to say Hyde hadn't seen titles he'd collaborated on with other authors hit those lists. He had.

Yeah, it's exciting. Listen, can I ask a favor?
Oh, sure. What can I do for you?

Her reply was followed with a devil-horned emoticon which made Hyde roll his eyes. Several times Hyde began typing, but then deleted his words. Choosing *how* to say what he needed to say to her was proving difficult.

Well, I guess it's not so much a favor as I need to tell you something. After we wrap *Tristan's Treasure*, I think it'll be time for us to both admit I can only do so much with my voice, and your male

leads are going to start melding together for the listeners.

The crack of the seal breaking on the third mini bottle seemed louder than it should have been, but Hyde was on edge while he waited. The dots weren't bouncing; she wasn't responding. Had she stepped away? He raised the vodka to his lips and closed his eyes to swallow it all down, but stopped short of swallowing when he heard the *ding*.

Are you... are you breaking up with me?

Hyde spluttered and spun his chair around, sending vodka down his front and all over the wall next to him. He was pretty certain she'd chosen her words with care, which meant this had already gone so much further than anything he'd imagined might happen. His panicked fingers flew across the keyboard.

***Tristan's Treasure* will be our last project together, Ms. Jackson.**

Again Hyde waited for a reply, his stomach turning into knots. He'd been in bed for the day, but had gotten up to use the bathroom. Why he hadn't taken care of business and gone straight back to bed, instead of deciding to check on things, now haunted him.

To think, I could be in my plush bed dreaming of all the naughty things I could do with Gypsy—

His forbidden thoughts came to a literal screeching halt when an awful din arose from outside. At the same time, his message box dinged.

I see. Well, we better make this one count then.

What the hell does she mean by that? Hyde was able to wonder half a second before the sound of tearing metal came from outside again, distracting him. For the first time since having them sealed up, he wished he had an upstairs window to look out of.

It just happens I'd been thinking about Tristan and Annabelle's story. I think it would come across much better if you

could partner with a woman to do Anna's part rather than just reading those. I know it means we'd have to start over, but, could that be done? I know it can, but are you willing to put your all into my baby?

His eyes skimmed the message as another grinding sound met his ears. Hyde had no time to sit here and debate with her. Something was being destroyed in his front yard.

Fine. Whatever. I'll talk to some associates and get some samples to you. Listen, I really have to run right now. We'll talk later.

Sending his reply, Hyde raced out of the room without waiting to see if she had anything more to say.

CHAPTER THREE

*A*fter a week of trying to survive on frozen meals and canned goods, Gypsy was fed up. If she could get her hands on some fresh vegetables, eggs, flour, and seafood, she'd whip up some pasta and fix one hell of a dinner. Years of working jobs in restaurants had broadened her kitchen skill levels. Besides craving real food, she also needed something to smooth the way toward telling Hyde about Tina. Time was running out before his brother would be bringing her niece back. In case Hyde had a bad reaction and flipped out, or felt the need to wander in the nude again, she thought it best he know before the girl arrived. Her niece didn't need to be exposed to such things.

Connie and Zeke had suggested it might be beneficial to allow everyone a probationary period, as it were. They'd made it clear that while they had faith in Gypsy's ability to do the job, they lacked faith in Hyde, or more specifically, his temperament, to keep her on for long. Inviting Tina back to their place in Charleston for a mini-vacation had been their way of making the transition as easy as possible. Their twin girls and Tina had hit it off splendidly, and Tina had straight-up begged to go when the offer was made. She'd talked to Tina every day, and hearing the girl sound happy again, like a kid should be, had been a balm on her heart.

It seemed Connie had gone ahead and posted the want ad which had started all this anyway, since a handful of prospects interested in her position had called in the last couple of days. So far, the calls had come mid-morning, and she'd been able to field them while Hyde slept. Gypsy didn't hold any hard feelings, but darn it all if the messages didn't keep ending up in the trash somehow.

Things were going as well as could be expected for two people in the early days of living together but operating on different schedules, so why not broach the topic of Tina with an over-the-top meal?

It'd be a piece of cake to take the car and run to the Food Lion in town, right?

Wrong.

It was too bad she never learned to drive a manual. All Gypsy had ever driven was an automatic. Of course, there was also the minor issue involving her lack of a valid driver's license—but no one else knew that besides her. If she were being technical, Gypsy had been asked if she *could* drive, not if it were legal for her to do so, therefore she had not lied to her employer. When her license had come up for renewal on her twentieth birthday, she hadn't been in the issuing state anymore, so never renewed it. Considering she'd been flitting around in the eight years since as she saw fit, Gypsy never secured a permanent address. Her sister had offered to let her use theirs for things like this, but she'd always turned it down, not wanting to be in anyone's debt. Ironic now, wasn't it?

Each time she tried to inch the old Ford Mustang forward out of the garage and another gear ground with a high-pitched shriek, Gypsy cringed. She was going to ruin the vehicle at this rate, which would not be conducive to endearing herself to Mr. Johnson. Her culinary skills had been stretched to their limits with the meager supplies, and because he was rather meticulous in tending his own needs, other than spot-cleaning the downstairs, there hadn't been much for her to do to impress him. Or convince him she was the right one for the job.

Taking a deep breath, Gypsy tried again. This time the car lurched forward, springing to life as her foot floored the pedal. Before she could get excited, utter fear washed over her when Hyde appeared in the direct path of the vehicle.

"Jesus Christ, fucking shitballs!" she screamed as she tried to sort out the brake.

The car stalled as it came to a stop about a foot from her boss. Her chest hurt where the seatbelt tightened across it. When she dared to look up, the livid expression on Hyde's face was enough to make her dribble in her pants a little.

His hands came down on the hood of the car, and his words could be heard through the Ford's windows as he yelled, "What the hell is wrong with you?"

Full of remorse, she took the keys from the ignition and then got out of the car. Her head was down as she walked forward. Gypsy winced when the keys were snatched from her hand.

"What did my car ever do to you?" The words,

spoken so close to her face, sent warm air across her cheek.

Telling herself she had to make this right, that she couldn't run away this time, Gypsy firmed her resolve and looked up into his dark eyes. Out here in the sunlight, she realized they were blue, not the brown she'd thought when seeing him inside, in the shadows.

"Are you going to answer me or stand there gawking?"

"I'm so sorry, Mr. Johnson. I just wanted to run to the Food Lion for some fresh ingredients to work with. And, well, I hadn't realized your car was a stick. I'm afraid I never learned. I apologize if I woke you." Hyde retreated a step, giving her some much-appreciated space, and Gypsy sucked in a breath.

Then, he started laughing.

"Of course, you can't. I swear, Zeke and Connie never think things through when they start meddling. Why would they make sure the person who's supposed to be my errand girl, or whatever, can drive? Oh, because that would make sense. Fucking hell. And that racket would've woken the dead."

"I can drive," she mumbled.

"What was that?"

"Technically, I *can* drive. An automatic."

"If that helps you sleep at night, sweetheart."

His derision was grating on her nerves. She'd made a *mistake*, something which was allowed on occasion. She was only human, after all. Gypsy was also tired, and as all the heartache and stress of the last month slammed into her at once, she blew.

"I told you the first day that nothing in my life is amusing right now, Mr. Johnson. I'm sorry I can't drive your stupid car. Guess what, I shouldn't be anyway, as I don't have a license, either. Because I don't have a home. Haven't had one for the last decade. Not since I turned eighteen and didn't look back. So, here I am, almost thirty years old and having to grow up at long last because my sister had to go and get bit by some fucking bug and die." Overwhelmed by the wall of grief which crashed down on her at admitting her sister's death out loud, Gypsy crumpled to the ground and started crying. "What am I supposed to do?"

Well, shit.

Hyde looked down at the crying girl—*woman*—and felt like the biggest dick on the planet. Part of her confession left him with questions, but he'd caught the gist. She'd had a recent death in her family, and here he was berating her like a monster.

"I– I didn't know. I'm sorry." He toed the ground as a hand went through his hair and he looked anywhere but straight at her.

She sniffled, wiped her nose on her sleeve, and lifted her chin to mumble, "S'okay."

A breeze picked up and shifted the black curls around her face, drawing his attention. It was mesmerizing how creamy her skin looked when the long locks moved back. The unusual shade of her glistening eyes, a grayish purple, left Hyde struck dumb by their beauty. This girl was trouble, with a capital T, and he found himself shell-shocked at the realization. It took him a moment to collect his bearings.

He sighed, and then extended his hand. "Maybe we need to start over?" When Gypsy quirked her head to the side with a baffled look, he grinned. "Hi, I'm Hyde Johnson. Nice to meet you. Can I help you off the ground?"

Gypsy's head went back, elongating her neck, and she laughed. Hyde's thoughts started to wander the line of her throat, but she settled down and smiled, then nodded at him while taking his hand, and he had to rein himself in. Hefting Gypsy to her feet, he invited her back inside.

"I'm going to go out on a limb and say that you probably have more to tell me. I've been given a good enough scare that it'll be hours before my heart calms down enough to sleep, so let's lay our cards out on the table and see how we can help each other, yeah?"

"That sounds great, Mr. Johnson."

"Hyde. Please. Mr. Johnson makes me sound like an old creeper."

She blushed. "Hyde it is, then. Um, I am sorry about the car. I should've waited and asked for help."

He waved his hand in dismissal. "It's not the end of the world, just an old car. Come on."

Gypsy was waiting out in the living room while he opened and closed every cupboard in the kitchen looking for tea or coffee. As he continued to come up empty, he had to admit she'd been correct about needing to go to the store. How long had it been since he'd put in a grocery order anyway?

Plan B it is.

Hyde returned to the den with a couple of take-out menus he'd found in the mail stack by the front door. "Point taken on the empty state of the kitchen. How about we order in for now, and after I've gotten some sleep," *and gotten this vodka out of my system*, he thought, "we'll see about driving lessons?"

There was such an abundance of gratitude in her expression when she turned to him, Hyde mused over what she'd endured in life for this small gesture to mean so much.

"So, um, pizza or Chinese?"

"I haven't had a good Chinese pig-out in forever," she hedged, her eyes starting to sparkle, "but it's barely eleven o'clock."

"So? Does the clock determine your hunger levels? One Chinese pig-out coming up. My phone is upstairs, I'll be right back."

With a soft giggle, Gypsy reminded him there were phones downstairs.

Feeling a tad embarrassed, Hyde shrugged and gave her a sheepish smile. A moment later, the phone he'd forgotten was behind him started ringing.

"Why, so there are." He winked at her as he picked up the handset. "Hush Studios, Hyde Johnson speaking."

A voice started chattering at him from the other end and his good mood evaporated.

CHAPTER FOUR

Now that he'd put the idea of Chinese food in her head, Gypsy found herself ravenous. Judging by the way his face was falling as he listened to the caller, she questioned if their plans were about to change, though. Then it hit her. On a normal day, he'd be asleep right now, and she'd be answering the call he was taking.

What if it's someone calling about the want ad? she fretted. Nervous, she started chewing on her thumbnail. Her stomach sank when his pacing stopped and he looked her direction as he spoke. Something was off in his voice.

"I'm going to stop you there, Justine, I believe you said it was? ... Yes, well, the position has been filled. I'm sorry about the mix-up. ... I'll get the ad pulled from the paper, yes. ... You have a good day, too."

Gypsy watched him hang the phone up, his demeanor the coldest she'd seen yet, and begin dialing a number. Since he didn't say anything to her, she waited. And then she tried to melt into the background when he let loose a verbal tirade.

"What the fuck is wrong with you? ... What do you mean, what am I talking about? Why are people calling my house about a job, Zeke? Tell me how my private, *unlisted*, fucking number got into a public forum. Explain that one, I'll wait..."

Oh, this doesn't look good.

While Gypsy knew he had a recording studio upstairs, she didn't know what it was that he did with it. The Johnsons had indicated discretion was needed for the job, but she hadn't considered how private he lived, or what placing that ad could mean. Until now.

"Fuck me, Zeke. Really? Why can't you keep your wife on a goddamn leash? ... Whatever. Save it, I don't want to hear it right now. Get the fucking ad pulled." He slammed the phone down, and Gypsy jumped.

"Is– is everything okay?"

Hyde's head snapped in her direction, like he'd

forgotten she was there. "No. Everything is not fucking okay. They're always sticking their nose in. Always. Why can't they just let me be? Let me live my life the way I want. They can have their prissy house with their sparkly pool and their perfect children, I don't care. I just want to be left the fuck alone."

"They're family. They love you." Gypsy found it hard to swallow.

She'd give anything to have her family back now. The selfish bastard didn't realize the treasure he had. Her appetite was gone, as was her determination to pave the way for Tina's arrival. Now wasn't the time. She wasn't sure it ever would be.

His eyes softened and he opened his mouth to say something, but closed it. It seemed he had no words to offer.

With a sad shake of her head, Gypsy went to her room and closed the door.

His head was buzzing, but not in a good way. The vodka was wearing off, the sleeplessness creeping in, and the guilt... oh, yeah, the fucking guilt was off the charts. A woman hadn't been able to make him feel so low, with so few words and a look, since his mother. He'd be angry about it except, like his mother, Gypsy was a hundred percent right in casting judgment upon him. Hyde was being an ass, no two ways about it. His family was simply trying to help. No matter how they jacked that up, there was no reason for him to take it out on Gypsy. She was an innocent bystander, with her own demons to bear, caught in the crossfire.

Hyde marched down the hall to her room and raised his fist, holding it poised to knock a few seconds before he chickened out. Instead, he turned and went back to the living room, where he grabbed the Chinese menu and ordered one of everything. The next call was to Fernwood Liquor. Tugging a decorative pillow down over his face, Hyde passed out on the sofa and slept until the doorbell rang an hour and a half later.

Groggy and discombobulated, Hyde signed for the food delivery, adding a hefty tip at the mere sight of all the boxes and bags. Maybe "one of every-thing" had been a tad excessive.

With a wide smile on his face, the delivery boy

waved and bowed, thanking Hyde to the point he wanted to yell at the guy to go already.

He was bringing in the fifth, and final, armful from the front step when the telltale sound of tires on gravel alerted him to another visitor. Relief washed over him as he narrowed his eyes and made out the familiar Honda belonging to Fernwood's driver. Another signature, and another exorbitant tip, "For your trouble," and Hyde was back inside, closing the door on the outside world.

For several moments he reclined against the front door, his eyes closed and his head back. Why did it feel like everything was starting to spiral out of control? A few short weeks ago, his life had seemed fine. He'd been content. His world had been quiet.

And I'd been every bit as alone as I am right now.

A few minutes later, he once again found himself standing in front of Gypsy's door, fist raised to knock. Like before, he lingered, unable to bring himself to follow through because he wasn't sure what he would say when—*if*—she opened the door. "Food's here," seemed too dull, but "Will you dine with me?" would make him sound like a conceited ass.

Spinning on his heel, Hyde fetched the case of Effen and carried it upstairs, to the recording booth, and restocked the bar. Helping himself to a double pour, he winced while the hot liquid worked down his throat to his empty belly. Thinking about the egg rolls and chow mein down in the kitchen, he decided at least *that* was one problem he could rectify.

He was opening the first container when his stomach growled loud enough to echo around the kitchen. What Hyde didn't expect, was an answering growl.

At her soft chuckle, he turned around and felt himself calm at the sight of her. Seeing the puffiness around her elven eyes hit him in the gut; she'd cried because of him.

"Sounds like we're both hungry, after all," Gypsy said, and a kindness in her voice soothed the hit he'd just taken.

Hyde reached into the cupboard and grabbed two plates, fetched some cutlery, and then stacked what food containers he could on the plates. He nodded over his shoulder at the boxed buffet when he passed Gypsy. "Grab what looks good and come on. I'm fucking starved." Not waiting for her, he went to the dining room and spread out his haul.

She joined him a few minutes later, a baking sheet laden with more food options in her hands. *Clever*, he noted as they filled their plates and began eating in silence. When their stomachs decided to talk to each other again, light laughter rang out from Gypsy while her porcelain cheeks tinged a soft pink.

"Oh, my god. How embarrassing. I'm sorry." Having managed to swallow her bite, she now cast her eyes everywhere but at him.

Hyde found himself wondering if other parts of her flushed as pretty, and had to shake his head.

"I'm doing it, too, ya know? Nothing to be ashamed of. Say, did you want anything to drink?" Vodka was sounding good to him right then. "I got you some soda..." he trailed off, ashamed to finish the sentence... *when I ordered my booze.*

"That'd be great. Thanks." She grinned and took another bite of teriyaki chicken, a little of the sauce dribbling on her chin.

Hyde stood and, using his thumb, wiped the sauce off her. He shocked them both when he stuck the sauced digit into his mouth and sucked it clean.

"Um..."

"You had some teriyaki there, sorry. I'll be right back."

Gypsy watched his hasty retreat with a dumb grin. Of their own accord, her fingers went to the spot he'd touched, and lingered there. The fluttering in her chest made her shake her head. She could *not* have an attraction to this man. Her priority now was Tina, which left no room for her to get involved in some silly fling that would end in disaster.

They always did.

She was selfish and stubborn, and her independence was what she thrived on. So, when her lovers let feelings bloom and started talking about tethering her to one place, her lone recourse became meanness. Whether by slipping away in the dark of night and vanishing without a trace, or showing them how awful she could be when backed into a corner. There'd been the odd occasion when the words falling from her lips on a tirade had shocked even her.

"I wasn't sure if you wanted it in a glass or out of the can, so I brought both." Hyde set her drink on the table with the glass of ice and returned to his seat.

"Over ice is perfect. Thank you." The drink fizzled and popped while Gypsy poured it over the cracking ice, and she smiled her appreciation. After a refreshing swallow, she shoveled another forkful of crab fried rice into her mouth before glancing up and noticing he was staring at her. She stopped chewing, and looked around. Forcing the bite down, she took another small sip of her soda to clear her throat, then asked, "What?"

"I'm sorry. Didn't mean to stare. It's just, I didn't think women ate like that."

Without missing a beat, she popped off, "I believe I did use the words pig and out." This earned her a hearty laugh. "Life's all about moderation, is all," she added.

Hyde's smile faded and she realized how shitty her comment sounded in light of his "excesses," as Zeke referred to his brother's mounting alcoholism.

"Hey—"

"It's all good," he said, cutting her off with a wave of his hand. "I'm glad you're enjoying the food."

"I am. Thank you."

"You don't have to keep thanking me."

"I—" Her mouth closed. Why was this so diffi-cult? Gypsy had never struggled for conversation around men before. Of any age.

Small talk, Gypsy.

"So, what do you record? If I can ask." She bit into an egg roll, appreciating the flavor exploding on her tongue.

Hyde's head tilted to the right as he regarded her. "Audiobooks."

"Wow. Really? That's kind of cool." Gypsy finished off the roll and took another drink, then wiped her mouth. "What kind of books?" she asked, trying to imagine his deep voice dictating some kind of self-help piece or a history textbook.

A wide grin spread across his face as he pushed the rest of a fried shrimp into his mouth, and chewed. "Mostly erotica," Hyde revealed after swallowing.

Gypsy choked on her lo mein, her surprised gasp having caused her to slurp a noodle into her throat. Hyde was on his feet and behind her in an instant, patting her back and then wrapping his arms around her. His clasped hands came up under her breasts, applying repeated pressure until she was coughing up the noodle.

"I'm sorry, didn't mean to offend you," Hyde said with a laugh and sat back down. "You okay?"

She swallowed down more soda. "No thanks to you," Gypsy teased. "And it takes a lot more than that to offend me."

"Oh?" An arched eyebrow emphasized his question, and her body warmed.

They were skating the line of flirting, and which way they fell would depend on her response.

"I'm not a child, and I've been around. You see things when you live on the road." Gypsy played it safe. "I've never listened to an audiobook, so I guess it wasn't a fair reaction. Just assumed those kinds of books would be read by a woman. I don't know why." She cocked her head to the side, considering. "Now I think about it, I guess it makes sense. Women are probably the focus of the fiction audio market, so why not reel them in with a sexy voice whispering all kinds of naughty things in their ears?"

"Smart lady," he praised. "I should clarify, though. What I do, it's not just reading. It's taking the words the authors have trusted me with and bringing them to life. Making each character real and distinct in the listener's mind."

As he spoke, Gypsy noticed a vibrancy she hadn't before, a passion. Perhaps there was more to Hyde Johnson than she'd first thought.

"So, you're kinda like a one-man band?"

"Sure. I guess you could say that."

A thought occurred to her and her cheeks warmed as she asked, "Do you, ya know? Make the sounds and stuff, too?"

Now, he really laughed. "Well, that depends on what 'stuff' you're referring to, but yes, I do some of that."

"Interesting." Gypsy's curiosity was growing with each question he answered, and she found herself wanting to sit and quiz him for hours. "What about the female parts? Your voice is too deep to pull those off, right?"

Hyde smirked and leaned in toward her. "You think I have a deep voice?"

"Don't you?" Warning bells started ringing in the back of her head. She leaned back.

"I partner up." He pushed the chair back and stood, his large palm reaching out toward her. "Come on. I'll show you."

Gypsy's heart raced as she took his hand.

hat the hell am I doing?

He knew taking her up to the booth and asking her to record with him, even if it were simple fun, was a bad idea. No good could come of having her voice in his data banks. Not true. There would likely be plenty of good coming if he had her voice saved. Hyde shook his head.

"Something wrong?" she quipped. Gypsy was looking around, her inquisitive eyes taking it all in.

"No. No, just thinking. Trying to decide if I should play something for you or not."

"Oh, please? I'd love to hear a sample." Her smile was radiant.

Hyde walked over to the equipment panel and

powered up the main console. After a few clicks, his playback speaker crackled, and then, his voice was filling the room.

"Tristan would have this woman tonight, and then he would leave. He'd purge her out of his system then hit the high seas with no plans to look back. He wouldn't think about her fiery hair. Or her luscious curves. There'd be other wenches to bring his rum and keep his tankards full. She moaned beneath him, bringing his wandering thoughts back to the warm body on offer, and as he locked eyes with her, he knew it was all a lie. There'd never be another woman like Annabelle."

Gypsy giggled. "Oh, my."

He'd never been present when another person listened to his work. Seeing her head tilt ever so slightly to the right as her eyes brightened with delight did something to him. There was a funny feeling in the pit of his stomach.

"So, yeah. That's my job. Recording words."

"No."

"No?" Hyde was puzzled.

"You had it right when you were explaining it to me earlier. You're doing much more than *just* recording words. I could hear it in that short example. You're performing, you just don't have a live audience. That was incredible." She smiled. "So, how does it all work exactly?"

It took him a moment to recover from her admiration and find his voice.

"Um, well, once the contract details have been sorted with the author, or their representative if the manuscript is owned by a publisher, then I'm sent a copy of the book. I like to do a quick read through to familiarize myself with the story and characters, and so I can take notes for possible sounds and music choices to enhance the audio experience. I'll put together the first fifteen minutes or so, sometimes the first chapter if it's on the shorter side, and send that in for review. Once they've signed off on my performance choices, voices and such, I get down to the business of recording."

"Fascinating. Do you always work alone?"

"Actually, no. Like I said, I partner up. Often, dual narration is preferred for these kinds of books. Something about them being a more authentic experience for the listener."

They both laughed.

"But whoever I pair with can record their parts in their studios, and then send them to me. I have high-end gear, so usually end up doing the final blending and editing in those cases."

"Would you record with someone in the same studio, if the chance came up?"

He'd never considered it, to be honest. That would mean he'd either have to leave the house, or he'd have to let someone in.

Like Gypsy right now.

"Maybe. I'd have to trust them. You know how I am about my space." He let the words hang in the air in between them, wishing he could read her mind and figure out if she'd caught what he hadn't said out loud: *I trust you.*

"Do you want to try?" Hyde asked, and her elfish eyes widened.

"Oh, I don't think—" she started.

"Come on, it'll be fun."

Gypsy still seemed uncertain, so he continued. "The author requested we start this project over, to a point, with a female reading Annabelle's parts. I told her I'd get some samples together, so I technically have her permission to share the manuscript. Wanna try?" he asked again. His heart was beginning to race at the possibility of hearing, no, *seeing* her lips form the wanton words Annabelle had upcoming.

"Sure, why not?" she relented, a sparkle appearing about her.

"Yeah?"

Nodding her head and laughing, Gypsy replied, "Yes. Let's give it a shot. It's just fun after all, not like you'll be using it for real."

Hyde burst into a flurry of activity, turning on the rest of his equipment, digging out an extra pair of headphones, and pulling up the manuscript. He clicked through to the page which picked up from the passage she'd just heard and pointed out where she needed to start. His movements came to a halt while he watched her eyes scan the words. Their gray color brightened to lilac, and when her cheeks flushed a pale pink, he almost came undone.

"So, um, you'll sit here." Hyde pointed to the stool in front of the mic and computer screen where he'd pulled up the script for read-along.

A light titter escaped her while she got comfortable and he helped her put on the head-phones. After giving her a quick rundown of what cues to look for, he pushed "record" and gave her the thumbs up to indicate the mic was hers.

Clearing her throat, she began. "*Annabelle felt Tristan's weight pressing her down, pinning her to the shabby mattress beneath them. She knew the Captain's bed was the best on the ship, but it didn't compare to the luxury she'd been snatched from."*

Gypsy threw her head back and laughed. "I'm sorry, I feel so silly reading this out loud."

He smiled. "You're doing great. Keep going."

She took a deep breath and refocused her attention on the screen, then resumed. *"The lost luxury was forgotten the moment the heavy weight of his manhood pushed at the needy spot between her legs. Each time he took her, he left her wanting more—"*

Another giggle stopped her reading. "Oh, gosh. I don't know if I can keep doing this..."

Gypsy turned those purple eyes on him and her words trailed off while Hyde moved closer, each step he took willing her to speak up. To stop him from what he knew he was about to do, but shouldn't.

His lips were seconds from brushing hers when she seemed to wake from her trance, and pulled back with a startled expression.

"Shit, I'm sorry," he mumbled, straightening back up and putting some space between them.

"I, uh..." Her eyes darted around the room before settling on him.

Right before she once again closed the distance between them.

He was no stranger to physical intimacy, but it had been a while since he'd shared it with another human being. Her lips were soft and pliable under his own, and as the kiss deepened, so did their desperation. She couldn't seem to decide whether to pull him closer or push him away, her hands clenching and unclenching in his shirt, so he tightened his hold on her and guided her into his bubble. When Gypsy's lips parted, his tongue didn't hesitate accepting the invitation.

Hyde saw stars.

When his chest began to burn, he broke the kiss. He was breathing heavy, gasping for air as he withdrew enough to look down into her eyes. Although Hyde kept the temperature in the studio cool—for the equipment and for staying alert—right now, he was hot.

"Gypsy?" He had so many questions, but couldn't make the words come out.

"I don't want to stop."

She didn't have to say anything else. Hyde bent at the knees and scooped her into his arms, then carried her downstairs to his bedroom.

To the bed that only he had ever slept in.

· · ·

Darkness had descended over the room when Hyde woke to Gypsy's low moans beside him. Her body was tense and twitchy. As the next moan raised in pitch and became a grimace-enhanced wail, he pulled her into his arms and kissed her forehead. To his great pleasure, she calmed at once. Hyde held her for several more minutes, until the call of nature made it impossible for him to stay.

Trying not to wake her, he wiggled out from under her warm body, then settled the covers around her so she'd feel held in his absence. His foot was crossing the threshold of the bathroom when Gypsy spoke in her sleep.

"It'll be okay, Tina."

It was said with such clarity that had he not known better, Hyde would've sworn she was awake. Shaking his head, he marched off to the bathroom remembering her words about nothing being amusing in her life, and wondering who Tina might be. He now had a bad feeling he'd fucked up bedding the girl—technically his employee—without knowing her whole story first.

Bladder empty, and able to breathe again, Hyde went upstairs, back to his recording studio.

Everything remained as they'd left it. Crossing over to the mic, he picked up her headset and put it on. He pushed a couple of buttons, and his ears filled with her voice, but more precious than that were the nervous giggles, the real Gypsy shining bright. A few keystrokes, and the file was saved.

He pulled up his social media, remembering to hide his active status this time, and was surprised to see Sami had been quiet. There were no waiting messages, nor had she tagged him in anything. Not one to look a gift horse in the mouth, he closed out of everything.

His usual standard operating procedure at this time of day was a shot of vodka and then recording all night, but when his stomach rumbled, reminding him he'd exerted himself earlier and that they'd left a bunch of food on the table, he reconsidered. Swinging his head from the mini-bar to the staircase, Hyde decided cold egg rolls sounded pretty darn good.

With a start, Gypsy woke and sat up. Cold air hit her naked, sweaty body, and memories flooded over her, warming her skin more.

Sure hands skimming her body. Gentle lips caressing. Everywhere. *Hot breaths, sticky skin. Cries in the dark...*

Her hand went out, searching for Hyde. When she found nothing, a brief bout of disappointment crushed her. Gathering the duvet around her, she stood to leave, and winced.

It'd been a while since a romp in the hay had left her sore. Heat flushed across her skin as flashes of her time with Hyde spun through her mind. She smiled.

Shuffling into the bathroom, Gypsy freshened up and then went to look for Hyde. Noticing the food on the table as she was about to mount the stairs, she dropped the duvet and made short work of putting it away. In the process, she noticed the egg rolls were gone, and felt an odd sense of satisfaction that he'd made the effort to go ahead and feed himself, *without* her shoving a plate in front of him and reminding him he needed to eat.

She still wanted to fix him that dinner. And, he still needed to be told about Tina. The afternoon, and then the evening, had gotten away from them, so she hadn't gotten the chance. As Gypsy considered her options, she came to a conclusion she might live to regret, but for now, was going to take a gamble on. Zeke and Connie would be bringing Tina back in five days. Hyde was finally acting like a person. Would it hurt to wait a few more days, maybe get to see more of Hyde's human side, before telling him about Tina?

Time would tell.

CHAPTER SIX

"*E*asy, easy... that sound doesn't mean good things are happening."

The past three days had been like a vacation. Hyde's demeanor had been the calmest, and most sober, she'd seen in the short time she'd known him. He'd taken Gypsy to the grocery store the morning after he'd taken her to bed, citing he had the next couple of days off from work while he waited for auditions to come in for Annabelle's part in the book. Until he had that sorted, there was nothing for him to do. With the larders stocked, and free time on both their hands, they'd been enjoying each other's company. They hadn't revisited their sleepover, yet, but there had been the occasional kiss or holding of hands and cuddling on the couch with a movie. It was like they both knew they needed to keep their hearts guarded. She was teaching him to cook, and he was trying to teach her how to drive his stick.

At least he's laughing, she thought as she stalled the car once again. They'd been at this for the last hour and Gypsy was convinced she would never get the hang of it.

"I hate this," she quipped and slammed her hands down on the steering wheel.

"Well, the car doesn't hate you, so stop hitting it."

She side-eyed him, but couldn't stay mad seeing the adorable grin he was throwing her way. "You're impossible."

"Maybe. Driving stick shift isn't, though. Come on. Try again. Both feet on the pedals, one on the brake and one on the clutch, shift it back into park before turning the key."

"I can't."

"You can."

Gypsy huffed, and pressing her feet into the damn pedals, she slipped the gearstick back then started the car. It turned over.

"Good. Now, ease into drive as you evenly let up on the clutch and push on the gas."

Holding her breath, she listened to Hyde's voice, focused on its warmth, and did as he said. The car moved forward, surprising her so much she almost shifted her feet in excitement, but caught herself after a small lurch.

"There ya go. Steady. Easy. Add a little more gas. That's right, you're doing it!"

And she was.

They were only moving down the driveway at about five miles per hour, but they were moving. Gypsy's confidence soared with her accomplishment and she braved a little more gas, getting them up to fifteen and second gear.

"Okay, the end of the drive is coming up, start slowing down, and take it back to first at the stop."

Her heart was racing inside her chest, scared this would be where she stalled out, but the car rolled to a smooth stop, then idled waiting for her next decision. Which was left, and out onto the road.

The first few upshifts were a little rough, but by the time they'd hit cruising speed, she had the car in fifth gear and everything was feeling good. Hyde continued to instruct from the passenger seat, praising her enough to keep her positive but not enough to distract her from driving. After a while, he pointed at an upcoming exit.

"Go ahead and get off there. Some of the best boiled peanuts around are sold out of Sally's Shack down this way. I'm thinking we grab a couple of pounds, then head home to crack some beers and watch a movie."

Sounded perfect to her.

The car shuddered as she parked and killed the engine. Gypsy hadn't realized how tight her grip on the wheel had been until she peeled her left hand from it. She laughed at her white knuckles.

"You did real good, Gypsy. Should be easy sailing from now on." His palm went up for a high-five, which she met. When he twisted his fingers into hers and kept hold of her hand as they started toward the shack, she didn't pull away.

"Howdy, folks. What'll it be today?" welcomed an older lady behind the counter.

"Afternoon, ma'am. Can we get two pounds, please?"

"Sure thing. Cajun or original?"

Hyde turned to her. "Your choice. I like both."

"Oh, please. Is there anything *but* original when it comes to goobers?" Gypsy scoffed, and Hyde laughed.

"You heard the lady. Two pounds of original, please." Hyde leaned toward the counter and stage-whispered, "Plus a half-pound of Cajun on the side."

Rolling her eyes, she chortled at him. "You could've just said you wanted both."

The drive back was uneventful. Gypsy, it seemed, could finally drive a stick shift. Next would be sorting a valid license. It crossed her mind to bring up the topic of Tina, but she didn't want to chance getting flustered while behind the wheel. Hyde carried the peanuts in, offering to get their beers while she went and set up a movie, her choice.

By the time they were cuddled on the couch, Gypsy had put the Tina discussion out of her mind.

Hyde stretched his arms above his head. "No matter how many times I see this, somehow I always expect the ending to change."

Instead of a verbal reply, he got a snore followed by a mumbled, *"Tina."*

"Gypsy." He nudged her with his elbow. "Hey, Gypsy, movie's over."

Her raven hair was tousled when she straightened up and blinked lazy, gray eyes at him. "Damn. One of these days I'll find out how this one ends." She yawned as he chuckled. "What?"

"Nothing. Do you need help getting to your room, or can you make it?" he asked as he stood and extended his hand to help her off the couch.

Gypsy waited until she'd been on her feet a few moments before stating she was good. Thanking him for the driving lesson and movie night, she waved goodnight and padded off down the hall. Hyde's eyes stayed fixed on her retreating form.

The soft click of the bedroom door shook him out of his trance and he looked around. Two weeks ago, he would've left the mess for someone else to deal with. Even if that someone was him, hours or days later. Tonight, he took matters into his own hands. Gathering the empty beer bottles, he deposited them in the recycle bin before cleaning up the peanut shells and dishes. With a last glance around the kitchen to see that all was in order, he flipped off the light and headed upstairs.

It had been easy to let himself get distracted by

Gypsy's presence. The downside was that he hadn't checked in on any of his business dealings for days now. Ten o'clock was early for him, so he had the whole night ahead to get caught up.

Of course, he was lying to himself.

Hyde's plan was to bury himself in work to avoid barging into the poor girl's room and burying himself in *her*. While it had been beyond wonderful, Hyde regretted what they'd done. He'd been too pent up, and had gotten too... enthusiastic with her. Although she hadn't said anything, his guilt-ridden conscience had kept him from pursuing her further. She would let him know when she wanted him again.

At least, he thought she would. She'd initiated the second round of their first kiss and asked him not to stop, after all—he knew she wasn't shy.

There was also the fact that she was his employee. Oh, and that she was still mourning her sister, who he assumed was this Tina she kept talking about in her sleep. The girl was carrying her own burden of guilt and he wouldn't press her.

For once in his miserable existence, Hyde was attempting to be a gentleman.

Stepping into the studio, he felt autopilot take over. His body and fingers went through the motions. Item by item, his equipment powered up and then his feet were carrying him to the mini-bar. A sharp scent of cucumber hit his nose as the clear liquid splashed into the shot glass. The icy vodka was poised over his mouth when he stopped, and set the glass back on the bar. To his surprise, he found he didn't want it.

No sooner had he pulled up his social media than the little private chat box dinged at him.

"Ah, Sami, there you are. How I haven't missed you." His eyes cut over to the shot glass, and he sighed as he clicked on the box then started typing without reading her prior messages.

Evening, Ms. Jackson.
Hyde! Where the hell have you been? It's been days.
I've been taking care of some personal business while waiting on the female auditions you requested.
Oh.
And?
I don't know yet. I just got logged on.
Okay, then. Well, I'm excited to hear what you come up with. How soon do you

think we'll be moving forward on the project?
That's going to depend on who has gotten back to me and their schedules. As soon as I have samples for you, I'll reach out.

Hyde noted the bouncing dots and cut her off so he could get to work. He wanted to knock out what needed doing and get back to his bed. And thoughts of Gypsy. His fingers hurried across the keys as he typed up the dismissal and then disconnected the messaging system. Before the window closed, he caught the start of her reply.

While the *"Goddammit, Hyde, don't you turn me off..."* didn't bode well for him, he couldn't find it in himself to be bothered by one of Sami's tantrums right now.

The next few hours passed in relative silence. Over on the mini-bar, the shot of vodka grew warm as it remained untouched. Hyde cleared out his email, made some requested edits on upcoming projects, and followed up on Annabelle's auditions. He'd received two, and while there was nothing wrong with them—he'd worked with Shannon and

Tracey in the past—Hyde kept hearing Gypsy's reading in his mind. The longer he thought about it, the more he was convinced he wanted to ask her to do the book with him. Who knew, maybe she'd learn a thing or two and pick up a new career.

To be sure his memory of how she'd sounded wasn't exaggerated, he pulled up the saved file and listened to it.

His head filled with images of the two of them recording together in the future. Becoming partners in the studio, and then, perhaps more, as they explored the inner workings of multiple romance novels. *She'd giggle, embarrassed, and her eyes would sparkle with faerie fire,* he started to think then laughed.

It echoed back, a reminder of his self-induced loneliness.

"Jesus, I need to get a grip."

Fifteen minutes later, Hyde had closed everything down. The last thing he did before shutting off the lights was pour the shot in the sink. An hour of yoga and a shower later found him crawling into bed, tired but content. He couldn't remember the last time he'd been able to say that.

CHAPTER SEVEN

"Man, did you go for a run or something to work up an appetite. There's so much food," Hyde said as he entered the kitchen, and startled her.

"Argh!" The pancake she'd been about to flip folded in on itself when Gypsy jerked at the sound of his unexpected voice.

"Sorry."

The word spoken near her ear made her jump again. He'd moved close enough she could smell the clean scent of soap. All her senses went on high alert while she glanced back at him. His hair was damp and messy, like a rough rub of a towel was all he'd bothered with, and he was shirtless. She didn't mean to stare, but the low-riding waistband of his lounge pants drew her eye. Gypsy took time appreciating the slight sculpting of his torso as she moved her gaze upward. When she reached his face, he was watching her, smug.

Busted.

"You're smoking."

Gypsy blinked. "Um, thank you..."

"No, behind you. Smoke."

A gasp strangled her as she spun around to find the folded glob of pancake blackening in the pan. What followed was akin to a comedy routine as she rushed to grab the skillet and dump the charring food. Water splashed everywhere when she shoved the mess under cold water, in addition to sending a billowing cloud of steam up in her face—all as the smoke detector started chirping overhead.

Once everything was under control and pancake cooking had resumed several minutes later, Gypsy addressed Hyde's initial question.

"Goobers and beer don't exactly count as a meal, so I woke up hungry. Bacon?" she offered, picking a crisp piece from the pile she'd already fried, and biting it while Hyde stared at her lips.

"I never say no to an offer of good pork," he quipped then reached past her to snag a piece for himself. Their bodies pressed together while he crunched on the bacon, and Hyde started to lean down.

The air left her lungs as warm lips found hers. Allowing herself a brief moment to enjoy his kiss, Gypsy had to force herself away lest she risk burning another pancake. Feeling flustered, she began rambling as she picked up the spatula.

"See how all the little bubbles have popped? That's how you know it's ready to flip."

He was still close. So very close.

"That's the trick, huh? I always thought my mom was some kind of magician because her pancakes came out perfect and fluffy..." he trailed off, a shadow darkening his blue eyes even as his brow furrowed.

"Hey, you okay?"

Hyde shook his head, then smiled. It was almost real. "Yeah, sorry. Hadn't thought about Mom like that in quite a while."

She didn't know his story, but his current demeanor and word choice hinted Hyde and Zeke's mother was no longer around. He seemed so sad all of a sudden, and if anyone could understand family deaths, it was her. Against her better judgment, Gypsy clicked all the burners off then turned to face him straight on as she asked, "What happened to her?"

Hyde stared down into her inquisitive face and wondered if he could do it. Could he tell this woman about his past? Did he dare open that box? He'd already caved and taken her to his bed, so, why shouldn't he? She hadn't shared his home long, yet her presence was bringing about changes in him. He knew it, and he was pretty sure she did, too. Taking a deep breath, he began telling her about the break-in, the neighbor finding their dog, Zeke coming to the school to tell him about their parents... all of it.

And she listened without judgment.

When he needed to pause, she didn't press. Somehow, she always handed him a fresh tissue each time he needed one. Although Gypsy held his hand, he felt her touch on his heart more.

By the time he'd let it all out, they'd moved to the living room couch, and he was drained. Hyde hadn't stopped at their deaths, he'd kept talking, sharing memories from much farther back, and then coming forward to explain how Hush Studios had come about. It felt great to remember the happy times. Far too much time had passed since he'd last allowed himself the luxury.

While he was sapped, he didn't want to stop what they'd started. Over the last couple of hours, she'd kept their coffee cups full in addition to bringing out the cooked food, which they grazed on while he talked. Hyde was enjoying the company and conversation, even if the topic wasn't the easiest.

"So, I've told you my story. What's yours?"

Gypsy stiffened beside him and her eyes started darting around, sending minor warning bells up in Hyde's mind. He reached for her hand, wanting to offer his support like she'd done for him.

"If you're not ready to talk, you don't have to, but I have to admit I feel pretty good right now. Best I've felt in ages if I'm being honest, and that's down to you. What I'm saying is, if you want to talk, tell me about your sister, I'll listen."

Her eyes teared up, and she blinked several times, trying to battle whatever was building inside her. Hyde was at a loss; he wanted to help her, not make her sad.

Damn this whole peopling thing.

There was a reason why he liked hiding in his studio. "Gypsy, I'm sorr—"

"No. Please, Hyde. You have nothing to be sorry about. It's just that I, well, I've been meaning to tell you something for a few days, but the time never seemed right."

"It's too soon for you to tell me we made a baby," he said, going for some levity as a nervous laugh escaped him.

Her lips pulled in and puckered. Scrunching her nose and puffing her cheeks, her eyes squeezed tight. He recognized it as a tremendous effort on her part to not cry. What fuckery had he stepped into? Before he could formulate the questions starting to brew in his head, the doorbell rang and, seconds later, chaos erupted on his quiet world.

Hyde had gone for the door, but halted in the foyer at the appearance of Zeke and Connie, their brood in tow, barging through it.

"Unca Hyde! We came back," squealed Randy as he made straight for Hyde. Under the unexpected ambush, all he could do was brace himself for impact as his nephew latched onto his legs and hugged. Although he never encouraged it, doing the opposite, in fact, with scowls and rough words, the boy adored him for some reason.

A low growl began building in his throat. "What the hell, Zeke?" His gaze raked over the large group standing before him, and stopped on a new addition. A young girl, who looked to be about the same age as Aimee and Ashlee, was hanging back, shoulders hunched.

Gypsy came around the corner then, and the girl came to life. More than a little stumped, Hyde watched as the two hugged each other, then felt his jaw drop when he heard Gypsy call the child Tina.

Ya gotta be fucking kidding me.

Tina was her *kid*, not her sister? Was this what she'd been about to tell him? And what the hell was this child doing with his brother's family? What had they been playing at? Had he been cast the fool all along? His ears began to ring and his sight started dimming as a steady throb settled in his cranium. All around him, everyone chatted like nothing was wrong. Like this was some big happy family reunion.

No one had closed the front door yet, so when another car approached, gravel crunching under its wheels reached the foyer, and the sound grated. Hyde didn't want any more surprises. What he wanted was to disappear upstairs and wait until they *all* cleared out of his goddamn space.

Marching toward the door, he came to a standstill when a blonde bombshell slipped from the new car, and waved at him.

"Howdy. My name's Kendall Rey," she called out with a heavy twang. "I'm here about the want ad in the paper. You wouldn't be Mr. Johnson, would ya?" Her arms crossed below an ample chest, putting her deep cleavage on display, as her hip cocked to the right.

Hyde drank her in with his eyes, starting at the shocking blonde cropped at her chin, inward to piercing green eyes, down over those jugs to a smooth stomach. The jutting hip curved into a long leg perched atop the sexiest red heel Hyde had ever seen. Casting a glance over his shoulder to where his family stood gawping at him, then to Gypsy, whose eyes filled with sorrow as they locked with his and made his gut twist, he made an impulse decision.

"Fuck you all," he barked then walked out the door.

He heard Zeke's voice shouting after him even as Connie's motherly pitch faded more with every step he took. Reaching the woman, he stuck his hand out. "Hyde Johnson. Can you read?"

Shock registered on her face for a moment

before she laughed. Hyde started to note it wasn't as lyrical as Gypsy's laugh, but dismissed the thought.

"Yes, sir. I can read. Write, too, on occasion," she teased.

His eyes ran up and down her body one more time, at close range, then he grabbed her by a wrist and started to drag her to the house.

"Wait. I need to close up the car."

He huffed, but let her go. It seemed to take her forever to bend over and lean in—at least he could appreciate the view—to retrieve her purse and keys then lock up. She sauntered back over to him and lifted her hand, offering her wrist to him with a saucy wink. A dark chuckle rumbled from his chest while he accepted, curling his fingers back around it. "Let's go."

Leading Kendall in, he ignored Zeke, knocking his brother's hand out of the way when he tried reaching for him, and then he tried to do the same with Gypsy. Her soft *"Hyde?"* managed to pierce his heart anyway. He'd been growing colder by the minute, and although a flash of warmth at the concern in her tone coursed through Hyde, the ice rebounded, searing away any reason to care right now.

Raising his voice with the full intent of rubbing it in, he said, "Kendall, let me give you a tour of Hush Studios." Behind him, silence reigned as he escorted the stranger upstairs.

Gypsy looked around the foyer, her heart sinking and her stomach starting to hurt. A flurry of emotions swirled around her in the ensuing silence. Elation to see Tina. Guilt Tina was here before she'd paved the way for her niece. Confusion at the blonde's arrival. Hurt over the way Hyde had ignored her, the final look in his eyes damning.

"Connie." Zeke's voice was low and controlled. Too controlled. "Why did that woman just say she was responding to the want ad? You canceled it a week ago, right?"

"Well, I meant to, but—"

"Jesus, Connie." Looking to the ceiling, Zeke covered his eyes then slowly dragged his hand down his face. "I can't say he's wrong to be mad this time."

"Aunt Gypsy, is this our new home?" The girl's question drew the attention of all three adults, and Gypsy pulled her niece in for another hug.

"I... well, I honestly don't know right now, Tina."

"Oh, sweetie. This is just a hiccup. We'll get everything sorted soon," Connie cooed before shouting at Randy, "Get away from those stairs, son. We're giving Uncle Hyde some cooldown time right now."

"Tell us, Gypsy. How has he been? Were things working out?" Zeke asked, calmer now.

"I thought so. Everything's been great. He taught me to drive and has been showing me how his job works. He's helped with meals, because I've been teaching him to cook. He hasn't been drunk since that first day you brought me here. We even —" she stopped, realizing she was about to blurt out that they'd slept together, too, and noticed both Zeke and Connie were staring at her. "What?"

"Are you talking about our Hyde?" Connie asked.

She scoffed. "Who else would I be talking about? It's just been the two of us." The couple exchanged a look, prompting Gypsy to ask again, "What?"

"That's great. That's all." Connie took Zeke's hand. "Isn't that great, honey?"

He nodded, unable to seem capable of putting

a sentence together as Aimee ran up to them, and asked, "Can Tina sleep in our room tonight?"

"Yay, slumber party!" chirped Ashlee, joining her sister.

"That'll be fine for tonight, but remember, girls, Tina will be living here now, so she'll be getting her own room once we get her settled."

Beside her, Gypsy felt Tina's grip on her waist tighten. For this little girl's sake, if not her own, she hoped Hyde got whatever stick had found its way up his ass, out. Of course, if she thought about it, this was all her fault really. Gypsy knew better than to let men get close.

It was her number one rule, and she'd broken it.

CHAPTER EIGHT

A couple of weeks had passed since Tina's return to Roebuck. Zeke and the gang left a few days after bringing her back, telling Gypsy to call if Hyde tried kicking them out. She, of course, had no intention of doing that. If Hyde told them to go, they would go. Gypsy didn't know where, but they would figure something out. In the meantime, she would lay low and have Tina do the same. School was starting in a couple more weeks, and the next appointment with her sister's lawyer, Ms. Stanford—to deal with the sale of the house— was coming up the first part of October. Much to Gypsy's appreciation, Connie helped her get down to the licensing office to take the road test before heading home to Charleston, which she passed with flying colors. It had been disheartening when Hyde hadn't shared the moment with her. He'd played such an integral part in preparing her. Thinking back on the driving lessons, and how much they'd laughed despite her frustration, brought a small pang of sorrow.

At least she and Tina had a roof over their heads and food to eat right now. She wouldn't lie to herself, the paycheck and security were nice. What wasn't so nice was that it was also looking like Hyde's blonde friend had moved in.

He hadn't said more than a handful of words to Gypsy in passing, but then, he'd gone back to his night hours, so she wasn't seeing him as much. She no longer bumped into him in the kitchen at lunch or shared a yoga session in the early morning; something she'd hated how bad it hurt her body, yet loved how it made her soul burst with energy. Kendall, the blonde, came and went during the day on occasion, but appeared to be keeping the same hours as Hyde. There was something about the coldness of her icy green eyes which bothered Gypsy. She couldn't put her finger on it, but she didn't trust the woman. Plus, dirty shot glasses were showing up in the sink again, and she'd taken a delivery the other day from Fernwood Liquor.

When she opened the door, they said Hyde had placed the order so she signed for it and left it at the bottom of the stairs. The box was gone the next morning.

What it came down to, was Gypsy biding her time. She was going to save as much of her paycheck as possible, while she was still getting one, and work on keeping life normal and stable for Tina until Gloria's estate settled. Once she could, she would get them a place of their own, and forget about having ever met Hyde Johnson.

And how upside down she went when he kissed her.

Tina pulled Gypsy from her internal reverie when she padded into the kitchen. She was dressed in a tank top and a pair of shorts, a towel over one arm and a worn book clutched in her hand.

"Whatcha up to, kiddo?"

"It's a beautiful day to go an adventure." Her niece beamed and shook her copy of *The Hobbit* at Gypsy. "Thought I'd get some sun," Tina added and grabbed a soda from the fridge.

"How about saving the soda for dinner," she suggested, pulling a thermos from the cupboard and loading it with ice cubes and water, which she handed over while Tina begrudgingly returned the soda.

"Fine." Tina's eyes rolled, but she smiled. "Thanks," she chirped and skipped off.

"Don't forget sunscreen!" The words were an automatic blurt, and Gypsy laughed despite herself. Seemed she was getting the hang of this whole mothering thing.

Feeling less pathetic after Tina's youthful infusion of pep, she grabbed the empty laundry basket and made her way through the house to collect any dirty laundry or misplaced dishes. It amused her how messy it was having a pre-teen around. Upstairs, the studio bathroom held used towels and the wet bar sink was full. Although it was none of her business, the sight brought feelings of disappointment. Before everything had gone sour, a new Hyde had been emerging. She'd only seen the vibrancy for a brief time, but she missed it.

She missed him.

Gypsy set about tidying the studio. A discarded hot pink bra wedged in the sofa cushions made her cringe. At the sight of the torn corner of a condom wrapper peeking out from under the couch she scoffed, thinking, *He wasn't so concerned about that with me,* before she blanched.

I wasn't so concerned either.

Her periods were always clockwork, so pregnancy wasn't a concern to her, but now she wondered if she'd been too trusting. How bad had she screwed up assuming a recluse didn't get "any" so he'd be free of disease? She'd seen two women who weren't family come through his front door.

He'd fucked them both.

It was getting harder to breathe. Her vision grew blurry. The room became too warm as her brain registered her name being called, then, nothing.

Seeing her upstairs surprised Hyde, and perplexed him, too, until he saw the basket and realized she was cleaning. Doing what he was paying her to do, her job. Still, as he watched from the doorway, he felt shame when she found the evidence of last night's escapades with Kendall. The woman was a looker, and while it had been fun making out with her or letting her blow him, he hadn't wanted to go any further. During their last recording session she'd kept the vodka poured, though; and by the time his words were slurring, she'd whipped those titties of hers out and he'd had no qualms about her pulling his dick out. It had gotten awkward when her sloppy mouth work only got him so hard, then downright embarrassing as a condom appeared from some-where on her person and she tore the packet open with her teeth. Trying to sheath a limp dick was never fun for anyone involved, least of all the owner of said limp dick, which is why he'd stum-bled off to bed at that point. He thanked the powers-that-be for small favors—at least Kendall had cleared out of the room rather than being found half-naked and passed out in his recording area by Gypsy.

One minute Gypsy was standing there, and the next, she was on her way to the ground.

Hyde rushed forward calling her name, but she was already in a heap when he reached her and pulled her body into his arms. He rocked her, brushing dark locks away from her face while whis-pering pleas to her to wake up. Which she did, moments later.

Confusion, shock, and then anger flashed through her enchanting eyes before she started thrashing and scrambling to get out of his grasp and stand up.

"Don't touch me," she hissed as she backed away.

He held his hands up. "I'm not. I'm not... are you okay?" When Gypsy looked at him without understanding, he explained, "You fainted. I, um, happened to be passing by."

Something told him now wasn't the time to confess he'd been standing there watching her.

"No, I didn't. Did I?" Now she appeared embarrassed as she glanced around then made a move to gather the laundry basket and make her exit.

Hyde stepped out of her way. "Maybe you should take the day off?"

"I'm fine. I just need to eat something, I'm sure. Dinner will be ready in about an hour," she mumbled the words as she inched past him then turned and disappeared from the room.

"Fuck!" Hyde exclaimed to the empty studio as he punched a fist into his opposite palm and then marched over to the wet bar. An icy shiver wracked his body when he yanked the fridge open to find the vodka was gone. Only an empty bottle mocked him from inside the chilled cavern. How was it already finished? He'd just stocked the shit two days ago.

"Hey, darlin'," Kendall crooned at him from the doorway. "Did you say something about fucking?"

Hyde clocked her swaying hips as she sauntered toward him and it took everything he could do to get to the bathroom before he hurled.

Although he was no stranger to excess, several years had passed since he'd last turned his stomach inside out because of an alcoholic binge. Trying to breathe and not drown in his own vomitus took most of his concentration. She was back there, somewhere, fussing over him, but her actions pushed his disgust deeper.

He was a fucking child. Gypsy was the best thing to have ever come into his life, and he'd shit on her by flaunting the first thing in a skirt to show up, in her face. What was wrong with him?

As the puking subsided, and the ringing in his ears began clearing, he stood and made his way to the sink. Cool water cleared the bile from his mouth, and then soothed his face and the back of his neck. It wasn't until he was toweling his face dry that he let his eyes drift up to the mirror, where he saw her watching like a timid mouse from behind him.

"I told you I wasn't interested, Kendall, and I don't appreciate whatever game you tried to play last night. We've got enough recorded for now. I need to touch base with the author to see if she even wants to use us as a team. Maybe it'd be best for you to go until details are ironed out on the project. I'll call you with a work schedule. If we get one."

Myriad emotions flickered in her green eyes before they closed to warning slits, and Hyde found himself gulping. The syrupy sweetness which dripped from her lips next, rather than the vitriol he'd expected, muddled him.

"But, I have nowhere to go. I cashed in everything I had to get here. Ya know, because the ad said room and board were included, so I gambled." She took a cautious step forward. "Call it woman's intuition, but I have every confidence the author is going to love what we've done. We make a great team, Hyde." Another bolder step brought her even closer and she stretched a lone finger out to tease the collar of his shirt. "Of course, I'd be happy to earn my keep in other ways, too."

Is she suggesting?

Hyde stepped back, out of her reach. "I don't keep whores."

"What?" Kendall's voice went shrill as her eyes flashed with surprise. "I was going to suggest you get rid of the other girl and let me take over that ad position. If the book stuff falls into place too, great, if not, so be it. How dare you insinuate anything else?" she asked while her face curled into a sneer.

The last dug into his gut. Life was easier when it was just him. There had been way too much coming and going in his world of late and, damn it all, he wasn't used to caring so much.

"Kendall, I'm sorry—"

"Save it," she snapped, becoming the second woman to storm out on him in the last five minutes.

His gaze turned longing as he double-checked the contents of the freezer. Hyde had never wanted a drink more than he did right then.

Something came over him, a need to be able to feel like he wasn't being watched or judged. Seeing to business first, he did as he'd told Kendall he would. After sending a selection of their recording to Sami—along with a sample of what he'd recorded with Gypsy, too, for some variety—he went to his room, grabbed his keys and wallet, and marched out of the house without telling a soul where he was going.

How could he, when he didn't know himself?

. . .

Hyde had been driving east on I-85 for almost an hour when the sun began setting in his rearview mirror. The fog cleared from his head as he looked around and realized he'd crossed into North Carolina when he saw the exit signs for Grover. While he'd set out thinking he just wanted to put distance between himself and his unusually crowded house, it was clear his subconscious had taken the wheel. Checking the hour on the old car's dash, he hoped he still had time before it closed for the night.

Although it had been a few years since he'd last come out here, Hyde guided the car through the lefts, rights, and lights of the small town like he drove the path every day. The simple iron gates stood open when he parked. Miss Daisy, the flower lady, wasn't in her usual spot, and Hyde spared a moment to wonder if her absence was because of the late hour, or worse. Had she passed?

Deciding he'd double the flowers the next time he visited, he steeled his back and marched through the gates of Grover Cemetery. His feet carried him forward, and within minutes he stopped to perch on the stone bench arranged before the marble headstone bearing the inscription:

Here lies Randall and Minerva Johnson
Partners in Life, Soulmates in Death
beloved parents and cherished friends

"Hi, Mom. Dad. Sorry it's been so long." Hyde's throat felt thick as he fought the sob threatening to escape.

he second time she almost cut her finger, Gypsy set the knife down and took a deep breath while gripping the counter's edge. He was infuriating.

No. Her reaction to him was.

She was not some naïve young thing who was clueless to the ways of men. That she'd allowed herself to think he might be different from the rest was careless, and therefore enough to berate and belittle herself without mercy. The curse words tumbling around her head would've made network television execs cringe.

Abandoning the food prep for packing her suitcase, Gypsy froze when she heard Tina's small voice behind her.

"What's going on, Aunt G?"

Shit. In her manic state, she'd forgotten her niece. Gypsy was letting the "old" her decide her current actions, which translated to get the hell out of Dodge. Except, she couldn't do that this time. Because this time she had responsibilities. She had Tina.

"Oh, hi. Are you done reading and sunning already?" Her brain raced for any excuse. "I was checking my stash of fall clothes. What do you say to some real shopping before school starts? We could call a cab to the bus station in the morning, then hitch a ride into Spartanburg and hit the mall." Even as she began voicing plans, a part of her brain was checking her bank balance and questioning how smart this was. She could take the Mustang, she supposed, now that she had a license again, but that would be relying on *his* graciousness. Something lacking of late.

"Um, yeah, it's getting warm out there and I figured dinner would be ready soon so I'd come in and clean up—"

"Shit, dinner!" Remembering the state she'd abandoned the kitchen in with her moment of panic, Gypsy found it all too much. She slumped onto the edge of the bed then buried her head in her hands.

"Hey, are you okay?" Tina came over to console her. "What's wrong?"

"I don't know how to do this, Tina," she confessed in a blubbery sob. "I can't even keep my own crap in order, how am I supposed to take care of you?"

Small arms slid in around her waist and tightened as Tina whispered, "We'll figure it out together, Aunt G. For what it's worth, you're doing great so far."

"Yeah?"

Tina pulled back and smiled. "Yeah."

"You're not so bad, kiddo, you know that?"

"And you're not such a bad aunt... when you feed me. I'm starved. When do we eat?"

Gypsy snorted hard enough a bubble of snot escaped her nose, which sent both of them into a fit of disgusted laughter as she lunged for the tissue box. Once she'd dealt with her nose, she nodded toward the door.

"Come on, we'll eat faster if you come help me."

"Let me change and put my book away, and I'll meet ya in the kitchen."

.   .   .

Gypsy had already washed and dried her hands, and resumed slicing the vegetables into thin discs when Tina joined her. "Hands clean before you touch anything," she directed her niece, earning her the eye roll Tina had perfected.

"Did it upstairs. Where can I start?"

Setting the knife on the cutting board, she assessed the kitchen and what was left to do. "The garlic spread should be softened, so you can go ahead and get the bread ready to toast right before we eat. The cheese is in the fridge still. After that, we'll need to get the pasta pot ready to go once this goes in the oven." Gypsy indicated the baking dish to her right. "The ratatouille will take about an hour."

"The rat what?" An expression of abject horror appeared on Tina's face.

Pointing at the pile of vegetables in front of her, Gypsy refrained from laughing and described the dish. The girl's face relaxed at the mention of tomatoes, herbs, and garlic.

"So, no rat, right?"

"I promise. Can you pass me the bowl of toma- toes next to you?"

Tina did as asked, and the two of them settled into a serene silence while they worked side by side. It took them about twenty minutes before Gypsy was sliding the artisan-looking pinwheel of veggies into the oven and setting the timer.

"Thanks for your help, kiddo. Did you have fun?"

"I did actually. Thanks for letting me help. Anything else I can do?"

"Nah, I'll handle the clean-up. You can take off, just be back in about an hour if you want your meal hot."

Not that it would taste bad reheated, or even cold, which is why it was one of her chosen recipes. So Hyde could fit a real meal into his nocturnal hours.

The quick, unprompted hug Tina gave her before she darted off left Gypsy with a warm spot in her chest, and she set about cleaning. Several minutes later, while humming to herself as she wiped down the counters, an icy shiver wracked her body, and she turned to find the blonde watching her from the doorway.

At being discovered, the woman straightened and plastered on a smile. "*Mm-mmm*, something sure smells good in here. Did you make enough for the whole class?" Kendall moved into the kitchen to help herself to a wine glass from the cupboard, a smarmy grin on her face.

Gypsy stood there guarded, reminding herself seven p.m. wasn't too early for an evening libation. Being truthful, she just didn't like how the woman had taken to moving about as if she owned the place.

"Tina and I don't eat much, and there's always enough to put away for Mr. Johnson to reheat when he gets up." Her answer was curt, Gypsy knew, the implication being she was Hyde's employee, not this woman's.

Kendall assessed her for the next few seconds, then drifted around retrieving and pouring her wine. "Too bad he's not here, then." Not another word was said as she wandered out of the kitchen.

With the woman gone, Gypsy relaxed and poured herself a glass of wine—since Kendall never offered while fixing her own. *Touché*, she thought and lifted the drink to her lips. The Gamay Beaujolais went down easy. Too easy.

She'd poured a second glass before the bimbo's last words registered in her head.

Setting the glass down, Gypsy slipped through the house quiet as a mouse, not wanting to let

Kendall know she'd gotten under her skin. Nudging the curtain aside by the front door, she could see the dark hole of the open garage. A bad feeling knotted her gut and she went back for her wine, Hyde's earlier expression as she repelled from his aide burned in her mind. There was no way she'd chased the man from his own home. Had she?

Where's that wine?

The hour was late when Hyde unlocked the front door. A faint scent of garlic and herbs hit his nose and his stomach growled, reminding him he'd not eaten. He flicked the lock on the door then stood and listened until he was satisfied no one was up and moving about. Toeing off his shoes, he made his way into the kitchen and over to the fridge.

She'd left the dim stove light on, so he didn't bother with the overhead. The prepared plate, wrapped in saran and fixed with a sticky note citing heating directions, touched him. Why'd she have to be such a good employee? He didn't recognize the dish, but a deep inhale convinced him he didn't care, because that scent told him it was going to be delicious.

She'd make an excellent wife.

He shook his head. For so many reasons he should let her go and put an end to this farce of a position his nutty sister-in-law had fabricated. Not to pursue Kendall—that was an issue for another day—but because he wasn't right for the likes of Gypsy. He'd be an anchor on her carefree outlook, and what a shame it would be to drag her into the depths of his despair.

The room filled with the odor of what he would best describe as "comfort" while the plate rotated in the microwave. Earthy, tangy, sweet, all the scents teased his mouth to watering by the time the low ding announced his food was ready. He got a glass of water, and a fork from the drawer, then pulled his dinner from the microwave and went toward the small dinette he kept in the kitchen area for his solitary habits, where he almost dropped everything.

Gypsy was hidden in the shadows of the corner, slumped over the table, her head on her arms. On the table were a wine glass and two bottles. All three were empty.

"Oh, sweetheart, you're going to regret that in the morning," he murmured and set his plate down. When he hefted her into his arms, she curled into him, her arms falling into a limp pile on her chest.

Her room was at this end of the house, but he had no idea where her kid—it still floored him that she was a mom—had set up camp. Not wanting to wake the child, he moved stealth-like down the hall. He debated undressing Gypsy, thinking to make her more comfortable, but then decided that she'd be more uncomfortable after, when she realized he'd taken the liberty.

Ducking into the bathroom, he came back with a towel and a cleaning bucket, which he set up next to the bed... just in case. Once Hyde had also put a glass of water and some saltines on her nightstand, he closed the door and went back to his meal.

It had gone cold again by then, but he enjoyed every bite.

Once his hunger had been sated he should've been exhausted, but after the day he'd had, Hyde was too spun up to sleep. He went to his office and turned on the computer to check on things. A quick run through his email cleared it, but also brought Sami Jackson's reply to the audition with Kendall. Hyde wasn't sure what to make of her enthusiasm. She claimed to love the sample and wanted the woman booked "no matter her rate." A small part of him had hoped Sami would hate it and provide him with the excuse to get Kendall out of the house, and he sighed. Why was it his problem she had no place to go again?

His thoughts twisted and turned in on themselves while he scrolled through the social media sites doing some basic marketing and checking listener reactions to the latest releases. After several minutes, he realized something was off. There were almost no posts, sales-related or otherwise, from Sami, which was odd for her. He clicked through her profiles, seeing if maybe she was giving more attention to another media platform, but no, it was like she'd vanished. It was curious, but he wasn't going to waste time wondering. She had replied to his email, so was alive. In all likelihood, she'd gone down the writer's rabbit hole, and would resurface when her next book was well underway.

Calling it a night, Hyde took a shower and went to bed thinking about the promise he'd made his parents that evening. It was time to let go of past regrets, beginning with letting people into his present.

CHAPTER TEN

Groaning and clutching her head, Gypsy rolled to her side and pulled the covers over her, but a second later her eyes flew open. An awful heat was surging through her body as her gorge rose, and it was all she could do to move toward the edge of the bed. As she scrambled, every part of her being knew she was about to get sick on the floor. Then she saw the bucket. A spare thought of gratitude passed through her mind while she grabbed the receptacle, and emptied her stomach.

It wasn't until after she'd showered that she spotted the crackers and water. Appreciation for her caretaker won as she nibbled on a salty wafer and vowed off ever drinking red wine again. *What* had she been thinking? Last thing she remembered was being in the kitchen, lamenting her sorrows with Pardon & Fils. Which begged the question, *who* had taken care of her, and how much of a fool had she made of herself?

Her stomach felt a little better, so she dared to look at the clock. She'd slept the whole morning away and a portion of the afternoon. Guilt drove her out into the house in search of Tina. In the kitchen, shame guided her hands in clearing the remnants of her little wine party from the table. She grabbed a ginger ale from the fridge, pleased to see the plate she'd left was gone—until it dawned on her Hyde had to be the one who'd gotten her from point A to B.

Damn her for being a tad offended he'd left her dressed.

Going into self-scold mode, Gypsy told herself she'd had a night of good fun with him and that was that. There wasn't going to be a repeat, so she needed to stop with the lustful thoughts about him.

An eerie feeling settled in when she cracked the soda open and it echoed in the space around her. Even as the bubbles tickled her tongue with the first swallow, she couldn't help thinking how quiet the house was.

Tina wasn't hanging out in the living room watching TV. Gypsy didn't find her out in the sunshine on the deck with her book either. Circling around to the front of the house, she steered clear of Kendall's car to check the garage. The Mustang was gone. Which meant Hyde hadn't come home after all, and someone else had seen her bacchian ways. Or, he had come home.

And left again.

Argh. I don't have time to worry about what he's doing. Where the hell is Tina?

Gypsy turned her focus back to the task of finding her niece. Inside, she paused at the base of the stairs. It didn't make sense that Tina would be up there, kids weren't allowed on the studio floor, but she was running out of places to look. Taking the steps two at a time, she was on the landing in moments.

Her eyes scanned the studio from the doorway. It was empty, and looked untouched from when she'd been in there the day before. Still, her feet moved forward while she found herself remembering time spent with Hyde. Listening, to reassure her solitude, she stepped over to the mic area and put on the discarded headphones. A finger hovered over the playback button, questioning whether she should do this. Unable to resist her curiosity, she pressed play.

Kendall's heavy drawl filled her ears, begging to be filled "deeper and harder," and Gypsy couldn't remove the headphones fast enough, only to realize she was still hearing the woman's voice with them off. Gypsy's head snapped toward the door.

"What do you think you're doing?"

"I thought I was alone."

"Clearly," Kendall sneered at her, and crossed her arms. "Well, what are you doing?"

"Nothing. Sorry, I was just curious." Gypsy wanted out of the room, but her exit was blocked. She inched away from the audio equipment, moving closer to the door, and Kendall. "I was actually looking for Tina. You haven't seen her, have you?"

"The brat?" she asked with a disinterested shrug, and Gypsy stiffened. "Yeah. Hyde took her somewhere."

"Do you know when they'll be back?"

Please say he's bringing her back.

She was trying not to panic, or let Kendall get to her. Hyde wouldn't haul her niece off without a word, would he? Where would he take her anyway? Gypsy was Tina's legal guardian and, as far as she knew, she hadn't done anything which could change that status. Unless she counted getting so drunk she passed out and couldn't remember anything. Still, if anything, she should be reporting *him* for kidnapping!

Before her thoughts got any wilder, the front door opened downstairs and the sound of Tina's excited chatter could be heard. Gypsy might've been mistaken, but she thought disappointment passed over Kendall's features.

Aw, is your game over, darling?

"Speak of the devil," Gypsy said, and then pushed past Kendall with a rushed, "Excuse me."

"How ya feeling?"

"Where have you been?"

"Aunt G, wait till you see!"

They all spoke at once, but it was Tina's exclamation at the end which won the bid for his attention as Hyde questioned, "Aunt?" His gaze went to Gypsy. "I thought she was your daughter."

Both Gypsy and Tina laughed.

"Oh, no. Well, I guess technically she is. Now.

I told you about losing my sister..." A quiet fell over the group while the words hung in the air.

The untold pieces of her story started assembling in Hyde's head, and he didn't know what to say. More things made sense now, at least. Sort of. Who was he kidding? Nothing made sense to him right now.

"So, uh, where were you guys?" Gypsy repeated, and Tina bubbled up with excitement again as she held up her bags.

After sharing her purchases, Tina bounded off to put away her things, leaving Gypsy and Hyde standing there facing each other. Her arms were tucked in against her frame, her body language protective.

"Thanks for taking her out today, you didn't have to. I was going to. Um, if you'll let me know what you spent, I'll pay you back."

All he'd done was get the girl a couple of outfits and some CD she'd gone on and on about while they drove to the mall, *Pray for the* something or other. The guy on the cover was a smooth-looking motherfucker, but Hyde had enjoyed listening to the album on the trip home anyway.

"I know. She mentioned when you still weren't up by ten. And it wasn't much, my treat."

God damn, she was beautiful when she blushed.

"Yeah... about that," she bit her lip, hesitating, "um, I had kind of a bad day. I don't usually do that, and I'm really sorry you had to see it—"

"Hello, pot. I'm kettle," he cut her off and stuck his hand out. "It was nothing. Not like I'm a saint or anything. Besides, after all you've done for me around here, it was the least I could do." His hand went to his pocket when she left it hanging, the other swiping through his unkempt hair before tucking into the opposite pocket. He rocked on his feet.

"Well, ain't this cozy?" Kendall appeared at the bottom of the stairs, a few feet from where they stood.

Hyde had no idea how long she'd been there, but he didn't like the way Gypsy reacted. She'd started to relax, her posture loosening, but now she'd gone rigid again, resembling a rabbit about to dart away at the first sign of danger. He wondered what had happened between the two women.

"If you'll excuse me, I need to go figure out what to fix for dinner."

He felt guilty for some reason, and put a hand out to stop her. Discovering her trembling under his palm alarmed him. "You're obviously not feeling well. How about a pizza and movie night?"

"Are we ordering pizza? I haven't had that in forever. Mom thought it was trash food." Tina had rejoined them and now looked between the two of them, ignorant of the tension hanging in the air.

Kendall snorted and made a comment about how fattening it was too, which jolted Gypsy into action, Hyde noticed with amusement.

"By the time it got here, assuming we can find someone who will deliver all the way out here, it would be cold. Besides, homemade is so much better. Wanna learn how to whip up a pizza pie?"

"Can we have ham and pineapple?" Tina asked.

"You bet, kiddo." Her head swiveled his direction and in a softer voice, Gypsy asked, "Would you like to come help, too?"

He'd started to follow the pair to the kitchen when Kendall's voice from behind stopped him mid-step.

"Hyde..." his name dripped like thick syrup from her lips, slow and messy, "did we get the job? Maybe we should get to work?"

Every fiber of his being wanted to turn around

and chew her out, but the logical part of him stayed the overreaction.

Gypsy had also stopped, and now watched over her shoulder, no doubt waiting for his decision.

"It's okay. Go, do what you need to. We'll let you know when the food is ready. Who knows, maybe you'll have enough done to join us for the movie," she said when he didn't move or speak.

"Sure, sounds good."

Her smile wasn't genuine as he turned to follow Kendall, but then, neither was the one he shared back.

Kendall wasn't subtle with her hind wiggles as she pranced ahead of him to the studio. He knew it was meant to entice, but he didn't feel like taking the bait. Hyde *was* considering switching up his hours, though. He'd liked being on the same schedule as Gypsy. Plus, if he switched to days, he was pretty sure there would be less temptation to partake in Kendall's games. The estimated finished length of this book was twenty-five hours. When it took an approximate two hours of narrating to finish one hour of audio book, he needed to plan on spending at least fifty hours with her. More if Sami wanted corrections or anything redone once they started submitting files to her for approval. A mere fifty to sixty hours was nothing in the grand scheme of things, right?

His thoughts suspended when he stepped over the threshold into his studio and found Kendall at the mic stand, headphones on, clothes off.

All of them.

He hurried to close the door behind him. "Fucking hell, Kendall. What are you doing? There's a child in the house."

The irony that *he* was concerned by this was not lost on him.

"I thought we could have some fun while we worked."

If he didn't shut his mouth, he was going to catch a fly.

"I didn't," he started, but stopped. "You have to put your clothes back on before anything else. I'll be downstairs."

Hyde fetched his laptop then all but ran down to the dining room. It took longer than he wanted to boot up the computer because he rushed typing in his password, twice, and had to slow the fuck down to not lock it up on the third try. Once he was in, he pulled up the highlighted word file for

Tristan's Treasure and sent a copy to the printer in the den. She had homework to do before they got down to the nitty-gritty of recording from page one —and the sooner she got started, the sooner this project would end.

Thoughts running a mile a minute while he was on his way to collect the printing pages, Hyde didn't see Gypsy until he almost knocked her over as she was coming out of the kitchen.

"Jesus. Sorry, Gypsy."

"I'm fine. Are you guys done already? You weren't up there very long. Pizzas are still about thirty minutes out..."

Pizza? Oh, that's right.

They were doing movie night. He'd suggested it. "Yeah. I mean, no, uh, I need to print the book out for Kendall," he said and moved toward the printer.

"Oh."

Had he imagined her face falling? Hyde wasn't sure, but felt the need to keep explaining anyway. "Sami Jackson, the author, chose her audition, so we'll, uh, be working together for the next couple of months or so."

For someone who earned their keep with a dexterous tongue, he sure was having trouble speaking. To be fair, he normally had a script to work from. Several of the longest seconds of his life passed while Gypsy regarded him, then gave a simple nod of her head.

"I assume she'll be staying on then. Will she be seeing to her own needs, or should I factor her into the meal planning? If I have to start doing her laundry and cleaning her space as well, we may need to talk about an increase in salary."

Hyde blinked. Her curt, matter-of-fact attitude was flummoxing. Especially since he'd thought they were moving forward, at least as friends, after their last encounter. Christ, women were an odd lot.

"Sure, whatever. Not like I started charging you for your niece moving in," he threw back at her, and she flinched.

He had no idea why he was picking a fight with her, but he couldn't deny her eyes were incredible when they flashed with anger. Even her pale, creamy skin seemed to glow from inside with her ire.

"Point taken. I'll be sure to shop separately for her and me from now on. *Your* pizzas will be ready soon. If you don't mind, I'll need to borrow the car tonight, though. To go get some food for Tina."

That she wasn't backing down, but giving back even dirtier, was turning him on. Girl was feisty, but this was escalating way too fast. It had never been his intention to drive her out, or hold the ability to eat over her head.

"Wait, Gypsy. This is getting out of hand. Of course, I'll cover the extra work, and no, you don't need to worry about Tina being here. She's a good kid. I'm sorry I let it go so far. I'm, well, I'm trying to work on some things—"

"There you are, Hyde," Kendall said as she joined them in the den and slithered up to his side, too possessive for his liking. "Am I interrupting?"

Gypsy smirked and tried to hide it by turning her head, but Hyde caught it.

They both knew Kendall was putting on an act. He had no one to blame but himself, though. If he hadn't lost his temper in the first place, Kendall never would've made it in the front door, let alone behind his mic.

As he looked between the two women who were turning his life upside down, he had to consider one thing. Did he want, or need, this project bad enough to deal with the potential disaster the next two months could bring? Steeling his resolve, he stepped away to collect the printout, tapping it on the table to even out the edges, and turned to Kendall. He didn't need the job, but flaking on it could be disastrous to his reputation and career. Call it a hunch, Hyde didn't think Sami would be all that pleasant, or professional, if he were to abandon the book.

"No, you aren't, but *I'm* done working for the night. This," he handed the thick stack of paper to her, "is for you. Congratulations on landing the part of Annabelle. Your first assignment is to read the book and get familiar with your character. If there are any words you aren't sure about pronouncing, or scenes you're uncomfortable portraying, we need to know before we record. My suggestion is that you take notes as you go." The goldfish look wasn't good for her, and he chuckled before he clapped his hands and directed his attention on Gypsy, saying, "That pizza smells great. When do we eat?"

In a huff, Kendall marched out of the room, and the rest of the evening went much better once the afternoon blip was put behind them. What, or where, she ate wasn't his concern.

Tina had chosen a predictable but fun movie, and the pies she and Gypsy made had to be the best damn pizza he'd ever put in his mouth. As the movie ended, Tina begged to put the sequel in. Gypsy looked at him, an apology in her eyes, and he waved it off, happy for the excuse to stay right where he was. Nestled against a beautiful woman.

By the time the second movie ended, the kid was sound asleep. Gypsy's gaze burned his back as he lifted and carried Tina to bed after she'd let him know which room the girl was using. Without a word, they slipped out after getting her tucked in, and made their way to the kitchen via the living room, where they gathered the dirty dishes.

An almost awkward silence settled over the pair as they moved around the kitchen putting the food away and tidying up from dinner. Now that the room wasn't filled with the scent of pizza cooking, he was catching the subtle scent of her shampoo as she flitted about. Each time the sweet odor teased his nostrils, he wanted to grab her, and kiss her. It was hardest to fight when they'd catch one another staring.

Hyde leaned against the counter, wringing the dishtowel in his hands and not wanting the night to end. "Can I get you a glass of wine or something?"

She scoffed with a vigorous shake of her head. "Thanks, but no thanks. I don't think I'll be having wine again any time soon."

"Sure. Of course." It'd been stupid of him to offer. Unlike him, she wasn't able to go right back to drinking after a binge—she wasn't an alcoholic. "What about a coffee?" he hedged, feeling almost shy.

"I don't know. It's a little late—"

"Hot chocolate, then?"

His enthusiasm earned him a light laugh before she relented, nodding her head.

"Can we have whipped cream?" Her eyes flashed amethyst for a brief second before calming to their unusual gray again.

He liked that she'd said "we," it meant she wasn't going to take her treat and scamper off to her room. Glad to have a task to busy his hands, he set about fixing the cocoa.

Stupid. Stupid. Stupid.

The warning bells were ringing, and Gypsy knew she should be listening, but she didn't want to. Not when the evening had been such a lovely one. Hanging out, just the three of them, had felt natural and right; like they were a family.

And it's thoughts like that which are going to get me screwed over.

Gypsy would drink the cocoa, say goodnight, and go to bed. Easy peasy. She was a strong, independent woman, not a giggling teen with fanciful crushes incited by lust, so she had this.

Right up until he flashed his dimpled smile at her while setting the steaming hot drink in front of her, and her will began to crumble.

Needing to avoid any kind of romantic atmosphere or conversation, she hurried to claim a topic.

"I know it's not any of my business, so you don't have to answer, of course, but where'd you go the other night? You know, when I..." her words lagged, she'd not meant to bring that up.

That line of talking could lead to questions about the *why* of what she'd done, which wasn't something she was going to admit to him. If he had any clue how much his presence messed with her head, it'd be a card he could play at any time. Gypsy wasn't having that.

"It's just that, you know, you don't go out much."

"I went for a drive," Hyde said after a reflective pause. "The house suddenly seemed full and

I needed some fresh air, so, I, uh, went for a drive."

Guilt slammed into her. While she knew it wasn't her own doing that landed her and Tina here, not really, it *was* her doing they'd stayed. Even after learning about Hyde and his preference to be alone. They were strangers in his home, and had encroached upon his safe space.

"Listen, I appreciate the job, but I get what I'm providing is not something you really need. It almost feels like a pity paycheck." Seeing the intent in his expression, she held up her hand when his mouth opened to protest her claim. "For both of us." His face screwed up in confusion, and she laughed. "You can deny it all you want, Hyde, but I can tell you care for your brother, even his meddling family. They care about you, and you know they were just looking out for you by bringing me in, but at the end of the day, you're a big boy. You could have told all of us to fuck off, and meant it." Gypsy's shoulders moved up and down. "You still could."

Jesus, the smile that transformed his face would stop traffic.

Or restart an angel's heartbeat.

"Has anyone ever told you you've got spunk?"

That made her giggle. "I've been accused of a lot in my life, being spunky isn't one of them."

Silence bloomed between them, stretching with each tick of the second hand on the clock behind her. She sipped her cocoa, waiting. For what, she didn't know.

"I went to see my parents."

Exhaling in relief—because she had to face it, she'd expected he was going to agree this wasn't necessary and ask them to move out—her head snapped up so she could study him. His eyes were cast down at his hands, where he picked at a torn cuticle. She didn't want to push, and instead took another sip of her drink then set the cup down on the table before reaching a single hand out toward him. Pausing to gather courage, Gypsy rested her palm on top of his hands before he could tear the cuticle more.

Tear-filled eyes turned her way, and the rawness looking back at her nearly broke her.

On their own they were hot messes. Together, Gypsy and Hyde were a disaster, and therefore likely doomed to failure before they could even begin. Like freshwater merging with salted, their environment became unstable and uncertain when they mixed. It seemed they couldn't catch a break either. Any time things started going smooth for them, something came up which churned their existence into chaos yet again.

To be fair, anything was possible in such murky waters, from new lifeforms being created to toxic algae and shark attacks.

"I don't understand. I thought they were—"

"Dead? They are. I went to their graves."

"Ah." *Of course.* She didn't know how to respond.

"It's been too long. After it happened, I stayed away about a year, but then made sure to get up to Grover every other week, on payday. There was a sweet old woman, Miss Daisy, who used to sell flowers at the gate, and I'd buy a bundle from her. They changed from time to time, but I always picked the biggest and brightest bouquet she had because that's what Mom would've liked." His voice caught and his shoulders shifted with a silent sob. "She wasn't there this time. I don't know if she's dead too."

"I'm sorry, Hyde. Maybe you just missed her?"

He hiccupped. "Yeah, maybe. It's been a while, though. And she was old to begin with. I guess I could check with the caretaker, see if she has a plot..." Hyde trailed off as a gray shadow settled in his eyes. "I don't know her name. In all the exchanges I had with her, I never learned her last name. I was always too wrapped up in my own issues to worry about anyone else."

"I'm sure we can find out," Gypsy said.

The smile he gave her said he appreciated the attempt, but not to feel obligated.

Another swallow emptied her cocoa mug and she stood. "I can't believe I'm saying this, but, I need to get to bed because it's a school night." She laughed, and his smile strengthened, becoming more genuine.

"Big day for Tina, I suppose."

"Me, too. I've always loved her, but never had to worry about her, ya know? Gloria was a fantastic mom. Now look at me. The once wild nomad child is setting appointments, keeping a calendar, and worrying about shot records." She scoffed. "Never pictured myself here, that's for sure."

Hyde's eyebrows pulled inward. "Do you not want kids of your own someday?"

Gypsy's reply was immediate, and cold. "Maybe when Hell freezes over. I'm not mother material."

"On that note, I think I'm going to call it a night as well." He stood and, collecting both their empty cups, took a few steps toward the kitchen before stopping and turning back to her. "Thanks for listening, Gypsy. You're a good friend. For what it's worth, I think you'd be a great mom, too."

Her mouth dropped open as she watched him leave.

hat woman doesn't want kids? Especially at her age.

Her declaration should've been fresh and intriguing, and instead, he felt personally attacked. Like she was saying she didn't want kids with *him*.

Had he lost his mind? Why should it bother him? If anyone had asked him the same question, he'd have said the same thing. Hyde wasn't made of parenting stuff. If anything, he was an overgrown kid locked in a man's body.

Mumbling to himself, his thoughts were going a million miles a minute as he rinsed the cocoa mugs and deposited them into the dishwasher. He wasn't hungry, but wanted something to munch on, so went rummaging in the pantry. Hyde was putting the finishing touches on a cheese and cracker plate when Kendall came into the kitchen.

"Oh, I didn't expect anyone to be in here."

As Kendall lingered in the shadows of the doorway, Hyde got the feeling she wanted to run, and chuckled. Wasn't he the lady killer, with his knack for sending women fleeing?

He'd never been good at anything "social," even before losing his parents. Their senseless demise cemented his outlook early in life—that people perpetuate chaos—so he had withdrawn into his childhood home, and himself. Discovering his knack for audio narration was the perfect solution, it allowed Hyde to exist in an anonymous and private world of his own making. Of course, that's where his troubles multiplied.

Because at some point, his self-loathing liquefied that world, blurring it into a swirl of words, deadlines, angry relatives, and blackouts.

Visiting his parents again had been cathartic, but he knew he had a long way to go. Credit had to be given where it was due, of course; it was because of Gypsy he'd even been sober enough to get there. Which is why he needed to steer clear of her... for her own good. He was bad news.

Sure, he was in the frame of mind to get his shit

together right now, but who could say how long that would last? Hyde could flip his lid at any time and be back at square one in a heartbeat, a shot glass in his hand.

"I was almost done. Just fixing a snack for while I get some work done upstairs." He picked up his plate and moved to the fridge for a beer. The icy cold of the can against his palm made him pause, but then he closed his fingers around the cylinder, thinking, *It's just one beer*, even as he looked toward Kendall expecting judgment.

For once, she didn't look like a harlot. Her short blonde hair was pulled back from her face with a wide cloth band and she was free of makeup. An oversized tee and slouchy sweats hid the body he knew was underneath. She looked softer, more approachable, and it jarred him.

Flashing her a smile, he quipped, "Kitchen's all yours. Don't burn it down."

The way she cowered back as he passed might as well have been a knife in his side and he stopped. He popped the can—being the experienced alcoholic he was, he'd perfected doing this one-handed—took a swig, and then turned back toward her.

"I'm sure I've fixed more than I can eat. Wanna

join me? I was going to work on some admin stuff, not recording, so you're welcome to bring your homework upstairs and hang out."

Her eyes were darker than he remembered when she stepped forward, but once she smiled, he wrote it off to her mood and the dim lighting.

"That'd be great actually. If you're sure? I don't want to intrude."

Hyde wasn't sure how he liked her in the role of a sweet damsel. It was disarming. If he'd only ever seen this side of her, things would be different, and he'd probably fall for it. Thing was, he *had* seen another side; in fact, he'd seen *all* her sides, in and out. He took another pull of his beer.

"I'm sure. The company would be nice."

"In that case, let me get my homework, Mr. Johnson." Kendall winked.

A wiser man would have realized the path he was treading, but he was tired, and alas, he'd only ever claimed to be passionate, not smart.

Who does he think he is?

Gypsy yanked at her clothes, peeling them off and tossing them at the hamper, which she missed.

What right does he have?

The curtain rings squealed against the bar, giving sound to her anger when she jerked back the material to start the shower. She cranked the nozzle toward hot, ignoring the ring she'd torn from its loop, and left the water to heat up while she stood in front of the sink. Her fingers gripped the counter as she stared herself down in the mirror.

So what if I'd be a good mom? I'm allowed to not want to be without getting the third degree.

Her eyes rolled back at her from the mirror.

Exaggerate much, Gypsy?

She took a deep breath, exhaling over a count of ten, and then looked in the mirror again.

None of it matters. Like it or not, I am a mom now.

And there it was. The acceptance of her new lot in life. Gone were the days of flitting along on her own schedule. No more harmless flirting turned into frantic one night stands filled with sweat and empty promises for her. An end to personal freedom.

Or, if I were to be an adult about all this, an end to the perpetual loneliness. Would it really kill me to open my heart?

Feeling calmer, Gypsy reached in and turned

the water off. Then, she retrieved her clothes and put them back on, skipping the bra and going commando. She finger-fluffed her hair, made a horse face in the mirror to check her teeth, and nodded.

They needed to stop tap-dancing around each other. Their hot-and-cold interaction thus far wasn't getting them anywhere. He'd indicated he'd made some revelations, similar to those she was coming to, so why couldn't they try to move forward? Together.

Gypsy strode from her room empowered with her decision. In her head, she tried to string together the words she would say when she joined Hyde, but stopped because she didn't want to sound rehearsed. Whatever she said, she wanted it to be from the heart.

The house was dark as she made her way through the downstairs, toward the other end of the building where Hyde's bedroom was located. She paused at Tina's door, listening for any indication of her niece being awake before cracking it open to peek inside. Her pulse eased at the sight of the girl sound asleep with *The Hobbit* in her hand, a halo of soft light from her bedside lamp framing her face. Gypsy tip-toed across the room and moved the book from Tina's hand to the nightstand, tucked the comforter in around her, and switched the lamp off.

Back in the hallway, she now moved with more purpose, excited to get to Hyde. Nerves tickled her stomach when she raised her hand to knock on his door, and she hesitated. Given their history, she wondered if she should she go ahead and go in. After all, she had come to surprise him.

Tossing her long black hair back, she straightened her shoulders, and then turned the knob. "Hyde?" she whispered as she entered the dark room.

When no answer came, she stopped moving and listened while letting her eyes adjust. His room was pitch black; he'd taken steps to ensure this as his days were usually spent sleeping. After a few moments, shapes and outlines began coming into focus, and she continued forward to find the bed still made, and empty.

If he wasn't here, there was only one other place in the house he could be. Gypsy could see now, and so she hurried back down the hall to the stairs, which she took two at a time. The door to the studio stood ajar as she approached, allowing her to hear the voices.

Thinking she was catching him working, she crept closer to see him in his element. A soft giggle had her insides turning to ice. Especially when she peered through the crack to watch almost the same scene from when he'd first invited her into the studio, unfolding between Hyde and Kendall.

Sat on the stool with the mic and headphones, while Hyde stood next to her, Kendall's head was tossed back as she laughed. His hand rested on her shoulder while he pointed out the prompts on the screen and which buttons did what. What shocked Gypsy most from the scene playing out before her was how casual Kendall looked.

She wasn't dressed to the nines or painted up like a doll. Her hair wasn't even fixed. Kendall almost looked like a different person, and judging by the way Hyde was interacting with her, he liked it.

Gypsy backed away, returning to her room, and her own bed, alone.

CHAPTER THIRTEEN

"Aunt G, wake up! I missed the bus."

Gypsy jolted upright in bed, and then out of it, as she tried to get her eyes to cooperate in seeing her niece. It took a few blinks and a couple of rubs before Tina came into view. At the sight of the big grin on the girl's face, she halted her rush to the dresser.

"What?"

Tina giggled. "Just messing with ya. But it is due in about fifteen minutes, so we are running kinda late."

"Shi–shoot. Sorry." Gypsy exhaled. "Crap. I still need to make you breakfast and a lunch, and —" she stopped when Tina stepped in and hugged her.

"Calm down, Aunt G. We're in this together, remember? I've already eaten, and I snagged a five from your purse for lunch." She chuckled when Gypsy clucked at her. "Come get a cup of coffee and walk me to the end of the drive? I'd like it if you'd wait for the bus with me."

How'd she get so lucky?

"You got it, kiddo. Gimme two minutes to get dressed." She hugged Tina back.

Exhaust plumed into the air as the brakes squawked their release while the bus pulled away. Gypsy stood watching until she could no longer see the yellow beast in the distance. All around her was quiet and serene. She sipped her coffee then started back down the drive with thoughts of her exceptional niece occupying her mind.

A flicker of movement in her peripheral brought her to a stop. Keeping still, Gypsy surveyed the wooded area around her. Her heart raced when she caught sight of a dappled pelt with a pair of pointy, tufted ears.

Frozen in awe, she was entranced as the black eyes stared back at her. The creature's mouth parted, revealing large canines as it tasted the air.

In all her roaming, she'd never been so close to nature. Dusted with red highlights and elaborately patterned, the bobcat was beautiful with its silver fur. She never would have seen it amongst the trees had it not been moving.

A low mewl threaded with the barest hint of that infamous eerie scream—the one which sounded like a woman being torn apart—broke the quiet of the morning and then the animal turned its back on her, disappearing into the surrounding camouflage of trees and shrubs.

Coffee spilled on her flip-flopped foot and Gypsy realized she was shaking.

She was still shaking as she got the shower started five minutes later, and by the time she'd covered herself with soap, she was openly sobbing as thoughts and images of her messed up life bombarded her.

The first day of her "new" outlook was going just splendid.

Not.

Hyde came to, afraid to open his eyes and assess his surroundings. He could hear her breathing next to him. Resigning himself to the inevitable, he rolled over and slid his lids open. As he studied her, flashes from the previous night came to him.

They'd gotten the first two chapters officially recorded with no shenanigans. It was during chapter three, where the first love scene occurred, when things had shifted in the studio. She hadn't been delivering a convincing enough Annabelle for his liking, and so they'd stopped to review the script. About the fourth time he beseeched her with the opening lines, something clicked. Neither of them had spoken, and she hadn't retreated from his approach. That first kiss had led them to here.

And he wasn't sure how he felt about it.

There had been nothing wrong with what they'd done. If he were honest, it'd been okay. Of course he'd enjoyed the physical aspects of it, the companionship, but it didn't hold a candle to his one time with Gypsy.

Stop that.

Hyde wasn't going to pursue the woman. He needed to let her be free so as not to break that entrancing spirit of hers, being attached to him would only drag her down. The last thing Hyde wanted was to see the purple fire go out in Gypsy's eyes, and the best way to ensure that was for him to remove himself from the equation.

"Good morning. What's got you looking so thoughtful this early?" Kendall blinked her bright emerald eyes and smiled at him from the pillow.

As she stretched, the thought, *Yay for distractions*, crossed Hyde's mind.

"Your voice sounds a little hoarse. Probably just not used to reading out loud yet. Some hot tea will help your throat and get you good as new in no time."

Her body tensed at his words, and then Kendall was rolling out of bed and bolting for the door as she rambled, "That'd be great. I just, um, I've really got to use the bathroom. Meet you downstairs." She vanished over the threshold.

Assuming she had to do more than pee, and therefore thankful she'd taken her business else-where—they weren't even *close* to being on that level—Hyde chuckled and went to handle his own transactions.

He was in the kitchen filling the electric kettle with water for her tea when he heard the front door slam, followed by the slap of flip-flops running across the wooden floors. Gypsy's bedroom door closed with a resounding thud a few moments later.

Concern had him running to check on her after first looking out the front door to see if there'd been an accident or something. When she didn't answer his knock, he cautiously entered the room. Finding the bathroom door closed, stubbornness drove him forward. He needed to know she was okay, but at the sound of an active shower, he turned and left. His will was only so strong, and seeing her naked would demolish what little he had.

Back in the kitchen, it was when he was fixing himself a cup of coffee from the already prepared brew that he remembered today was the first day of school for Tina. Gypsy's dramatic entrance didn't seem so dramatic anymore. She'd probably gotten up late, shuffled Tina to the bus in her pajamas without a morning pit stop, and then had to rush back in. Hyde needed to chill out already.

The kettle whistled then, and he'd added the hot water and honey along with a tea bag to a large mug by the time Kendall joined him.

"Thanks, darlin'." She beamed at him, her now painted lips and coifed hair even more off-putting than before.

Was that why she'd had to run off to the bathroom? He nodded and brought his coffee cup to his lips. Hyde was finding he preferred his women natural. After taking a sip, he set up his exit.

"Well, I've got some admin work to do, since we recorded last night and I didn't get it done then, so, if you'll excuse me..."

Kendall took a small taste of her tea and started to scrunch her nose up, but seemed to catch herself as the look of displeasure morphed into a cagey smile. "Oh, okay. I'd thought we'd snuggle some more..." Hyde remained stoic, and she moved on, "or not. Lunch, then?"

"Yeah, we'll see," he hedged and moved on past her.

She was latching on too tight, too fast, for his liking. In the morning light, he was beginning to think he'd really fucked up.

Again.

It took Hyde about an hour to do his basic admin before he pulled up the chapters they'd recorded last night to work on. After running them through his own edits, so that they were to his exacting satisfaction, he uploaded the files to the system then composed a quick update to Sami on what was included, how he and Kendall were working as a team, and what his current expectations for the project were. There were still some menial tasks he wanted to get checked off his list before he went and did a workout, but he needed a break first. He used the bathroom then went down to the kitchen for a coffee refill.

Kendall was in the living room, her attention buried in her phone while some morning talk show blared from the ignored television. He shook his head at her entitlement, and kept going.

Part of him still wished Sami had chosen the sample he'd sent of him and Gypsy, but the logical part knew they were too volatile for that. They could barely make it through a few hours without it turning sour or becoming awkward in some way by the end, which wouldn't be good for a business project. No, it was better that he do this with Kendall.

Or a long-distance associate, the way I usually fucking do it, he thought with a grimace, and then found himself once again longing for the peaceful solitude the old schoolhouse had once provided. He had no idea how his home had become Grand Central Station this summer.

Back in the studio, a barrage of recent memories, all including a certain smiling raven-haired beauty, hit him, reminding him it hadn't been *all* bad. Driving, chasing each other with the hose while washing the car, kitchen mishaps, boiled peanuts, pizza, and movies...

The ding from an email alert made him sigh as he released the indulgent thoughts to fade away. Seeing that it was from Sami surprised him. Given how quiet she'd been of late, he'd thought it would take a day or two for her to respond. At the very least, more than the ten minutes it had been since he'd sent the chapters. She couldn't have logged in and listened to them this quick. Not sure what to expect, he opened the message:

Hyde! It's perfect. I love the two of you together. Can't wait for more.
Xoxo, Sami

Short, sweet, and oddly enthusiastic. He didn't get time to analyze her words much longer because his computer began dinging and chirping with alerts from the various platforms he had open—Facebook, Twitter, LinkedIn, and more.

"What the..?" Hyde clicked on the first couple,

and then a few more. "Has she lost her goddamned fucking mind?"

She'd just social media blasted the world that her "lusty linguist lad" had manned up, at last, and made an honest woman out of her. And her profile picture, which he'd never seen her change, now displayed a generic "out of office until further notice" graphic. What the fuck did that even mean?

A shiver went up his spine as he looked around his office and thanked the powers that be that he lived in seclusion. Seemed Ms. Jackson was leading the crazy revolution these days, and he didn't want her anywhere near him.

CHAPTER FOURTEEN

For all intents and purposes, Gypsy had to admit life had been ambling along smoothly. She didn't know if she would call herself happy, but she could say she was doing okay.

Tina was settling into school. If she was having any issues handling her grief, she was hiding it from Gypsy. She doubted the girl would do such a thing, though. They'd made a pact with each other to always be honest, no matter how sad, a few days after school had started. She'd come home in tears because her friends weren't her friends anymore.

Over chocolate milk and rice crispy treats, they'd "analyzed" and "diagnosed" the situation in terms Tina could handle. It all boiled down to the nature of a small town. Tina was the only orphan they knew, except she'd grown up with these kids. Before passing, her mom had tucked them in on sleepovers and made pancakes and shit in the morning. Everyone was feeling Gloria's absence, not just Gypsy and Tina, and young as her friends were, they didn't know how to process their emotions or act around Tina now.

Not every day had been peachy, of course, and they'd worked through those with a movie and popcorn or wasting a couple of hours just being girls. While it wasn't Gypsy's thing to be made up or worry how her nails looked, Tina was developing a knack for, and enjoying administering, beauty treatments. Besides, if it made her niece smile, then she didn't mind being a living doll for a short while.

Interaction with Hyde, when it happened, was amicable and brief. They said what they needed to say to each other and then cleared out. A couple of times, one or other of them had lingered, as if they wanted to talk more, but the silences would become uncomfortable and then they'd both flounder or mumble something incoherent before darting off. Money was left in the glove compartment of the car for when she needed gas or groceries, and an envelope with her pay had been slid under her door every Friday morning.

Her one certainty was that even now, after almost a month of this weird regimen they'd all fallen into, she still couldn't be in the same room with him without her heart trying to race its way past her ribs.

As for Kendall, well, the two women had managed to avoid each other altogether. Without discussing it, they'd figured out the other's schedule enough to prevent confrontation, and their physical paths didn't cross. Sure, Gypsy would come across the other woman's dirty dishes or partially completed laundry—which she felt was a direct sabotage, to delay Gypsy from getting her work done—and it would make her cuss under her breath because she didn't *want* to clean up after Kendall. It was just so much easier to handle whatever it was than to worry about a face-off. She didn't want to be petty.

Gypsy got up each morning and walked Tina to the bus, then came home and ran through the chores. It never took more than a couple of hours, and then she would start dinner, or run to the store if groceries were needed first. Once Tina was home, they kept to their end of the house for the evening, the pair of them retiring to bed before Hyde's nocturnal habits had him rising. For the time being, it was working.

The bobcat hadn't returned. Some days, she wondered if she'd ever seen it at all.

Now, though, she recalled the piercing stare of the cat. Gypsy tried remembering the power coming off the animal in its stealthy confidence. Even when it'd been discovered, that it had turned its back on her had said more than human words ever could have. The creature had known all along it had the upper hand, and it had let her go.

She wanted to experience that surety now, that lack of fear. Gypsy was craving confidence to get through her meeting with the estate lawyer in a few minutes. After today, all the documents would be finalized and signed, and she would one hundred percent be Tina's legal guardian. The lawyer had offered to set up a stipend to be drawn from the estate for Tina's "care and upbringing," but Gypsy had refused. One way or another, she intended to take full responsibility for her niece's needs. She wouldn't spend a cent of the girl's inheritance from her parents. Instead, Gypsy had requested it all be included in the trust Gloria had prepared for Tina after they'd lost Jim, Tina's father.

Checking her appearance in the rearview mirror one last time, she nodded and got out of the car. Shoulders back, Gypsy marched into the building.

It took a conscious effort to close her mouth.

Across the way, Ms. Stanford appeared distraught. She fidgeted with her pen, clicking the end tab over and over, and shifted papers about on the desk, reordering them.

"Why do I need to designate any kind of beneficiary? I don't have anything to designate," Gypsy challenged. "And if I did, I'd think it should be obvious by now. Tina. Gets. Everything."

This was supposed to be an in-and-out appointment. That's why they'd had three telephone calls prior to this, so that Ms. Stanford could get all the info she needed and have the documents ready to go. Gypsy wasn't going to be allowed time to get frustrated, or have to deal with those damn encroaching tendrils of guilt and grief that loved to reach for her in her weakest moments.

Yet, here she was, her chest tightening with the

first traces of a panic attack. Gypsy didn't want to adult, and a blanket fort sounded perfect right then, but she had no choice.

"Actually, you do, Ms. Hartford. Your sister saw to that." A shaky hand offered a piece of paper Gypsy refused to look at.

"No. I told you on the phone, I don't want any help from Tina's money. It all goes to her trust for when she's older."

Ms. Stanford set the paper back down on the stack in front of her, and then made direct eye contact with Gypsy.

"You misunderstand. Gloria established a savings account for you about ten years ago. Tax laws have allowed her to make an annual maximum gift deposit into that acco—"

Gypsy started choking. She might not have been formally educated, or all-knowing when it came to financial stuff, but she knew the basic tax rules. It'd been in her best interest to stay on top of them as she floated from job to job. Knowing how much she could earn before the back-breaking work wasn't worth the effort had kept her moving. And evading a tax bill.

Prior to 2002, that annual tax-free gift had been ten thousand; with inflation, the limit had only gone up each year. Then there was the inter-est. Which meant this woman was telling Gypsy she had a bank account somewhere with over a hundred grand in it.

"Ho– how much?" she asked in disbelief.

The lawyer shuffled through a few more papers and then held up a sheet. "This is a couple of months old, closer to the date of—"

"Thanks." Gypsy took the bank statement and began scanning it.

The bolded six-figure number at the bottom made her mouth fall open again. If her sister weren't already dead, she'd kill her now.

CHAPTER FIFTEEN

*O*ut in the house, a door slammed, and then another. Hyde sat up in bed and reached for his phone to check the time.

"Aunt G!" rang out, followed by shoes thumping across the wood. *"Aunt G, where are you?"*

His body was moving before his head caught up to what he was doing. By the time he'd pulled on some lounge pants and a tee, the cogs in his brain were starting to process what facts he knew: it was four in the afternoon, Tina was home from school, and Gypsy wasn't here.

Why isn't Gypsy here?

He checked his phone again, marking the date this time, and then he remembered. It was the first of October, so she was meeting with the lawyer today. It'd been on the house calendar Gypsy had suggested they put in the kitchen to avoid any conflicts.

That worked well, he thought with a chuckle then shuffled out. He caught up with Tina as she was coming in from the back deck.

"Hyde, do you know where my aunt is? She always meets me at the bus." Her bottom lip trembled, and as he looked closer, he realized her eyes were filling with tears, too.

"Hey, it's okay, kiddo. My bad. I should've been up there to meet you, but I forgot to set my alarm." The kid was normally pretty laid back, so he wasn't sure what was going on.

She nodded, and bit her lip to calm the quiver. "Where is she?" Tina asked.

Hyde softened his voice as he answered, "She had to go down to Columbia today, remember? To meet with your mom's lawyer." Her expression said she didn't remember, so he took her into the kitchen to show her the calendar.

He was flummoxed for a minute when it was still on September; that meant he'd remembered the date from when Gypsy had first shown him the calendar. Not because of a reminder, but because it'd been important. Hyde shook his head then flipped the page to October and pointed to the box labeled the first, where Gypsy had inked in the meeting.

"Oh, that's right," mumbled Tina.

"You know how these things go. Appointments run late, traffic sucks, that kind of stuff. I'm sure she'll be home soon."

A single tear escaped and rolled down her cheek, and Hyde started to panic. He wasn't prepared for this.

"Are you okay? Did something happen?"

"Yes. No." Tina sighed then melted into one of the stools at the island counter and dropped her head on her arms. "I don't know."

"Tell me about it over a snack?" he offered, thinking how Gypsy always offered something comforting from the kitchen when problems came up.

Tina's eyes brightened with her small smile, and Hyde gave himself a mental pat on the back. Maybe he was better prepared for this than he thought.

"Oh, my god. That is so cool!"

With the headphones on Tina had no idea how loud she was being, he knew, and Hyde laughed at the girl's exuberance.

It was a grand improvement on how she'd come home, even if it had been total chance they'd ended up here. After a peanut butter and jelly sandwich and a glass of milk each, she'd opened her backpack to get started on homework, and a notebook labeled "The Legend of Nogard" had fallen on the floor as she pulled her stuff out. Once Tina had explained it was a story she'd started writing, about an orphaned dragon, he'd had the brilliant idea to bring her up to the studio and play around with recording what she had so far.

He was finding he needed the distraction, too. It wasn't like Gypsy to blow off her responsibility to Tina like this, and the later it got, the more worried he was getting she hadn't called to at least check-in.

"Yeah, kid. You might have a gift for the whole writing thing. Seriously, your story's not half bad." When she shook her head, he pressed on in a Yogi Bear voice, "Oh, come on. I have read a few more books than the average bear. I think I would know."

Tina giggled. "No thanks to you. It's your voices that made it better than it's ever sounded in my head." She high-fived him, adding, "Dude, you should've been the one voicing Smaug. Your dragon is so much better than that British guy."

"Thanks." He ruffled her dark hair—it wasn't midnight black like Gypsy's, but it was close. "You should think about showing that to your English teacher or something. I bet there's somewhere you can submit it."

"Why would I want to do that?"

"I don't know. Why wouldn't you? You ever hear of that Paolini guy? He published a series about dragons while he was a kid."

"I don't know..."

"What's Gypsy say? Has she read any of this?"

Tina's face fell and then she looked away. "No."

"Well, why not? I mean, if you can let me read it, you can let her, right?"

"It's not that. It'd be kinda cool if she'd read it and let me know what she thinks. I just don't want to bother her. She's trying so hard to keep it together, for me, so I try to give her some room at night."

He wondered if the girl had any idea how advanced her level of understanding was. Hyde knew what Tina was referring to, had seen it in

Gypsy himself, but hadn't taken the time to comprehend it so succinctly.

"I promised her I'd tell her if I got sad about Mom and Dad, and I do, on the really bad nights. Most nights it's not too bad, and it works to just write. I know the story is basic, but it lets me get out of my head. If that makes sense?" Tina continued.

"Yeah, kid. It makes perfect sense. We all have our ways of coping. You write."

I drink.

Deciding it was time to lighten things up, he changed gears, positive she'd love to talk about *anything* else.

"So, are you going to the Halloween carnival?"

Like most rural areas, it was normal to hold holiday celebrations in town, as a community gathering. The houses were too far apart, with too little lighting on the roads between, for it to be safe for door to door trick-or-treating. He and Zeke had always looked forward to the annual carnival hosted by the school, and to this day, for this one holiday, he still dug out his mother's decorations.

She cringed and shuddered. "No. I don't think so."

"Have you got something against the best holiday of the year?"

"There isn't going to be a carnival."

"I'm sorry, what? There's always a carnival. It's tradition. How can there not be a carnival?" His body slumped as he wondered what was becoming of the world.

Tina shrugged her shoulders. "Something about not enough volunteers, I think. They are going to do a dance that night, though."

"Can you still dress up?"

"Yeah. There's rules about what will and won't be allowed. Doesn't matter. Halloween sucks and I don't want to go."

Hyde couldn't believe what he was hearing. Didn't every kid love Halloween?

"What? How can that be? You've got candy. And costumes. *Friday the Thirteenth* marathons and caramel corn, and all the things that go bump in the night."

"My mom never really liked all that. She was worried about the sugar first, and what might have been lurking second, and so we didn't celebrate."

"That's a real shame. Every kid should experience a proper Halloween as a rite of passage into adulthood."

The stink-eye she gave him caused an unexpected guffaw to bellow from him.

"Okay, so maybe that's a bit of an exaggeration. I'm not kidding about the experience, though. I think you should help me decorate this weekend." Her eyes widened, but he was on a roll, his excitement taking over. "And if you'll allow me, I'd be honored to escort you to that school dance. Assuming some younger stud doesn't steal you, of course." As Hyde bowed, he got the first real smile he'd seen from Tina all afternoon.

She was quick to catch on and play along. "You'll have to ask my aunt. That would be proper, after all."

"Of course, miss. As you wish." His tone now matching the Dread Pirate Roberts, he bowed again.

"Well, well, well. What's all this?"

Hyde's smile vanished as he turned to the door. He'd been having such a great afternoon with Tina, he'd forgotten all about Kendall. Her whereabouts, let alone her existence, hadn't even crossed his mind.

"Kendall, hi."

The blonde strolled over and draped an arm over his shoulder, around his neck. "Hello, Hyde," she drawled, and then waved her other hand around while saying, "I didn't know children were allowed in the studio now."

Hyde shrugged out from under her arm, and stood. Although it wasn't any of her business, given their recent intimacies, he felt some sympathy toward her, so answered, "Tina's hanging out with me today while Gypsy takes care of some personal business."

"Ah. Isn't that quaint?" Kendall's nails seemed more interesting to her than making eye contact with him.

This was getting ridiculous. When it was the two of them, she actually wasn't so bad to be around. She was almost calmer, less "on" all the time, and they'd been knocking out chapters of *Tristan's Treasure* ahead of his anticipated schedule. He could sort of understand why she acted like this around Gypsy, but it was absurd she felt threatened by, or that she was in competition with, Tina. The girl wasn't even a teenager yet for crying out loud.

"What have you been up to today?" he asked Kendall, wanting to diffuse the volatility of the room.

"This and that. I went in to town to do a little shopping."

"That's nice. Find anything good?" He was surprised to hear she had extra funds for this, considering she'd given everything up to come work for him—according to her.

She scoffed. "Please. It was nice to get out and about, but this town doesn't offer much. It's so quiet and lonely around here. I still need a real city fix, and soon." Her fake laugh sent up the hairs on the back of his neck.

Now *that*, he found funny. The house was huge, and sat on five acres of mostly wooded land.

For a country girl, she should have felt right at home here. Any provincial person he'd ever met tended to avoid large groupings of buildings, not run toward them.

"I meant to ask when I first came up, but got sidetracked with the chicken over there," she nodded in Tina's direction, "have you heard anything about the car?"

Hyde glanced over at Tina, who had gone quiet. The carefree smile from moments before now a fading memory, her lips were drawn tight, as was the rest of her face. Such contempt and loathing rolled off her, he had to take a step back and suck in a breath.

If looks could kill, man.

"What car?"

"Well, yours, of course."

He had no doubt the long lazy blinks she did over the next few seconds were meant to appear innocent, but his gut was sinking. Fast. Snippets of conversations where Gypsy had complained about Kendall being devious—not downright mean, but annoying and childish with some of her antics around the house—came back to him.

"Explain."

"You haven't heard anything then. Oh, bother."

Kendall stepped toward him, extending her hand and placing it on his forearm like she was about to tell him someone had died.

Gypsy spent a good fifteen minutes sitting in the car, in the parking lot, outside Ms. Stanford's office. The whole time, she stared at the paper in her hand, her mind too blown to function. She'd woken up a pauper, with maybe fifty bucks in her bank account, and in the space of a few hours, she'd become richer than she ever dreamed she would. While Gypsy didn't plan to use the money any time soon, if ever, she could see the benefit of having it accessible.

"Dammit, Gloria!" she cursed skyward.

Even in death, her big sister was still adulting better than her. Gloria was probably out there in the ether somewhere, a smug grin on her face right now. Could *she* be any more pathetic? Gypsy sighed.

Right. Let's do this.

After rereading the directions the lawyer had written down for her, then double checking them against her phone, she started the car. The bank needed her to come by with a ton of certified paperwork in order to release the funds into her possession; all of which had been conveniently ready and in an oversized envelope by the end of her appointment, thanks to Ms. Stanford's assistant. All she needed was to present a valid ID in person, which she now had thanks to Hyde.

Well, working for Hyde.

She spared a second to wish he could've somehow accompanied her today.

Depending on traffic, the trip to Columbia and back could take up to four hours, so she wanted to wrap up all her business while she was already here. If she hurried, she'd make it before the bank closed for lunch. Otherwise, she'd have to hang out, and would never make it back to Roebuck before Tina got home. As she followed the audio directions coming from her phone, her eyes darted between the speedometer and the clock. A ticket would suck, but so would being late for her niece.

She gave the car a little more gas and upshifted.

The tires let out a squeal, and she locked up the clutch as the car lurched into the only available parking space she could find. It was, of course, the farthest from the door. Gypsy grabbed at her purse and the envelope, and jumped out of the car. She'd taken half a dozen steps when she realized she hadn't locked the Ford, so she shuffled back, yanked the door open, pushed down the lock, and then ran across the lot.

Sweat dripped down her back while she stepped into the cool air conditioning under the watchful eyes of the guard on duty.

"Good morning, ma'am."

"Morning." Gypsy nodded. "I need to see someone in accounts?"

The guard pointed at a sign-in sheet.

"Thanks."

Once she'd scribbled her name and reason for visit on the form, she took a seat in the lobby. She started digging in her purse, looking for her phone so she could shoot Hyde a text. This shouldn't take too long, but just in case, she wanted to send him a heads up. The idea that Tina might come home to no one expecting her had Gypsy's stomach curling up in knots.

"You've got to be kidding me," she murmured as she came up empty and realized she must have left it in the car. It had been wedged into the console so she could hear the directions.

Gypsy eyed the door, wondering if she dared attempting to go get it.

"Ms. Hartford?"

She turned at the sound of her name being called. "Yes? Hi. Yes, that's me." A smile in place, Gypsy followed the employee back to his desk.

"Nice to meet you, Ms. Hartford. I'm Thomas, personal accounts manager. What brings you in today?" he asked and folded his hands in front of him.

The envelope *thwapped* as it landed on the desk.

"I understand my sister left me an account. I'm here to claim it."

"Well, let's see what we can do then." He turned to his computer and hit a few keys before opening the envelope. Once he'd entered her name, and a few more keystrokes, his eyes widened, as did his smile.

"Ms. Hartford, can I offer you a refreshment? Fresh cookie, or a sparkling water perhaps? We pride ourselves on making any visit from one of our preferred elite members pleasant and satisfying."

Preferred elite member?

"I'm good, thanks. If we can just get this done, I'll grab some lunch before heading home." She was bouncing the balls of her feet, and in turn, her knees went up and down. One finger already stung from a torn cuticle because she had to pick at something when she was nervous.

"Very good."

Clacking filled the silence as Thomas input what information he needed from the forms she'd provided. After about ten minutes, he looked up and smiled.

"If I can get a copy of your ID, we'll have the forms printed for your signature."

Gypsy handed over her license.

Thomas looked between her and the card, and back again. "Late bloomer, I see."

"I'm sorry?"

"Oh, I was simply noting that you seem a little old for having just gotten a license." He tapped the issue date printed on her ID.

"I spent a lot of time moving around. Never stayed put long enough to get one until recently." For some reason, she felt like she was on the stand and being given the third degree.

"I see."

With each tap of a key on his keyboard, her

impatience and anxiety ratcheted up another degree. While she watched, he lifted the desk phone to his ear, punched in a number, followed by a verbal string of numbers, her name, and then a few grunts and murmurs in response to whomever was on the other end.

"I'll be right back. Just have to go get those off the printer." Thomas sauntered from the office, leaving her sitting there staring at the walls.

Twenty minutes later, she'd signed everything and he'd given her copies, along with new customer pamphlets and other assorted items for the account. They shook hands as he wished her well on her drive and told her the best way to get back to I-26, and then Gypsy all but ran from the building. She needed to get home.

Gypsy was halfway across the parking lot before she realized there were two police officers peering through the windows of Hyde's car, and she slowed. An irrational fear gripped her, convincing her Thomas had stalled her inside, while he called and reported her. There might be a tax year, or two, she'd conveniently never filed. Although, to be fair, she hadn't been back to those states.

A deer frozen in headlights, the officer nearest

her had to speak to Gypsy multiple times before she realized she was being addressed.

"Ma'am, is this your car?"

The question perturbed her. What did that have to do with her finances?

"Yes."

"Can we see your license and registration, please?"

Even as the officer in front of her asked the question, Gypsy noticed his partner removing a set of handcuffs from his belt. She blinked back inevitable tears.

CHAPTER SEVENTEEN

"Pick up, pick up. Come on, Gypsy, pick up already," chanted Hyde while wearing an invisible path on his deck pacing back and forth.

Kendall had slinked off somewhere. He might hear her out later, but right now, it was best that she'd disappeared.

Hyde relaxed his jaw then dared a glance toward the sliding glass door. Sure enough, Tina stood there watching him, the anxiety clear on her face as she waited for him to find out something. Overhead, a loud clap of thunder announced an approaching storm.

He attempted a wave.

She attempted a smile.

He went back to listening to the phone ring through to Gypsy's voicemail—again. His next call was to the operator, who he asked to put him through to the Roebuck PD.

No less than five times did he explain – to a new person each time – he wanted to "unreport" a stolen car, because there'd been a mistake. At last, he reached someone who seemed to have a clue, Candace, and after she put him on hold to see what she could find out, he let the conversation with Kendall replay in his head, to see if he could make sense of how this had happened.

"It was such a lovely morning, so I put the windows down and pulled my hair back so the wind wouldn't blow it around too awful. I was almost to town when it dawned on me something had been off before I left. By the time I got over to Cavalier Way, I knew what it was. The garage had been open and your car was gone."

Hyde blinked at her, praying he was wrong about what her next words were going to be.

"So, I went straight to the sheriff's office and reported your car stolen." She beamed. "Isn't it a good thing I noticed?"

His hands balled into fists at his sides. "Fuck."

Hyde had no idea if Kendall had maliciously orchestrated this disaster, or if it'd been an actual attempt to help. It hurt his head to think a person could be so dense, though. Why the hell wouldn't she have called him before going to the police? And if it'd been intentional... he shook his head. None of that mattered right now. All he was worried about was making sure Gypsy could get home.

"Mr. Johnson?"

Candace came back on the line just as the first fat drops of rain started to fall, so he took the call inside.

"I'm still here."

"Well, I've got good news and bad. Which do you want first?"

His whole torso moved and his shoulders dipped with his deep sigh. Call it a hunch, he didn't think anything she had to tell him was going to be good. "Ease me in?"

Candace laughed. *"Okay, then. Well, I found the case file in the system, and it had been dispatched statewide..."*

The way she trailed off implied Hyde was

supposed to understand what that meant, but he wasn't firing on all pins right now.

"Which means?"

"*So, the good news is that the car was found. In Columbia.*"

He exhaled, feeling relieved. With any luck, that meant she'd made it to her appointment.

"*But the woman driving it, uh,*" there was a shuffling of paper in the background, "*a Gypsy Hartford, was taken into custody.*"

"Oh, shit."

"*I'm assuming you don't want charges pressed against Ms. Hartford?*"

There was nothing else he could do, so Hyde laughed. "No. No, I don't." Under his breath, he mumbled, "A certain Ms. Rey, however, I could throttle."

Over the next little bit, Hyde answered questions. They were going to need to see his ID and get some signatures in order to clear the charges and release the car back into Gypsy's possession. Plus, there was the small matter of the impound fees.

Of course, there is.

Seeing that he was without any means of transportation, because the car was in Columbia,

Candace offered to send an officer out to the house. He supposed he could've asked to borrow Kendall's car, but that would've meant talking to her, and Hyde was nowhere ready to do that, not and be able to remain calm.

Tina had stood beside him once he'd become animated in his conversation with Candace. Now, she sat there listening and offering him comforting smiles despite how scared she must have been. Hyde could've kicked himself for not thinking sooner about how Gypsy's disappearance would affect the girl.

"Thanks for everything, Candace. ... You, too. ... Have a good one, bye."

He turned to Tina. "Well, kid, your aunt is fine. She's probably going to be madder than a wet hornet by the time she gets here, though. How about we order a pizza for dinner?"

The garage door rumbled and creaked as it rolled down on its rusty hinges. Gypsy blew the hair back from her face and prepared to trudge across the yard to the front door. Most days the detached garage was cool, tonight, as the rain poured down like a final statement to her day, she wished she wasn't about to dodge puddles in the dark.

Nerves, exhaustion, and the storm had turned the two-hour drive into over three. She hadn't dared go a single mile over the speed limit, when visibility would even allow it, for fear of another run-in with South Carolina's folks-in-blue. This afternoon had been enough of an experience to last her a lifetime.

A beacon, the porch light gave her a target to focus on and, holding her stuff against her chest and ducking her head, she bolted into the chilly rain. Halfway across the yard, she ran into something, banging her knee and causing her to drop her purse.

"Shit, dammit, fuck me!"

Yanking on the straps, she looked up, and then impulse took over when she saw what had stopped her. Gypsy wound her purse up and slammed it down on the hood of Kendall's car multiple times. Several small dents could be seen in the next flash of lightning.

It shouldn't have been in the middle of the fucking yard.

Not wanting to assume anyone had waited up for her, she entered the house with as little noise as possible. Light poured from the kitchen, and off to her right, the TV flickered in the dark den. Gypsy stood still, listening while she dripped on the floor.

Met with silence, she tip-toed over to the den and peeked in. Hyde and Tina were asleep on the couch while the movie they'd put in played on without them. As much as today had sucked, the sight melted something inside her. She rested her head against the door frame, and smiled.

As if he sensed her there, Hyde stirred and opened his eyes. A soft smile stretched his lips, revealing his dimples, as he waved at her. She waved back and nodded toward the kitchen, assuming he'd follow.

Which, he did.

"Hey." He yawned, and moved to cover his mouth with his hand. "Sorry."

Gypsy waved him off. "Hi."

They stared at each other, waiting for the other to speak first, and then both spoke at the same time—

"Thanks for being there for Tina today."

"I'm sorry today went to shit for you."

After a stilted chuckle, Hyde offered her pizza leftovers.

"That, and a beer, actually sounds fantastic

right now. Let me get out of these wet clothes and get Tina to her room, and I'll be back to collect."

"She's almost as big as you, let me take care of her while you get changed."

"You sure?"

"Yeah, I got it. Go on."

She nodded and made for the door, stopping to look back and say again, "Hyde, thanks for today. For looking after Tina."

"It was nothing."

Gypsy gave her head a little shake. "No. It was everything," she said, and then walked away, taking the last word with her.

An hour later, Gypsy was stuffed and feeling no pain as her head buzzed with her third beer. After today, she'd said fuck it. No doubt she'd be sorry in the morning, but for now, she was enjoying the low jazz coming from the sound system, the fading taste of tomato, cheese, and greasy meats on her tongue, and Hyde's company. He'd been recounting how he and Tina had spent the afternoon, the plans they'd made for Halloween.

Gypsy laughed. "Gloria got that from our

mom. My mother had to be one of the most paranoid women on the planet. Dad tried to get her to lighten up, but she was forever worried about germs and strangers, and things she had zero control over. I think it's why I went the way I did. All that oppression drove me to want to hit the road and explore what life had to offer." She finished off her beer and set the can on the coffee table. "It's also why I've never wanted kids of my own."

Hyde had been paying attention to her, of course, but now his focus seemed to heighten. They'd treaded this path before, and it had gone wrong.

"There are enough fucked up people walking around this planet. I don't need to add more by trying to pass on my screwed up ethics."

Before he could respond, Kendall came around the corner. Their eyes met, and Gypsy could feel her hate. She'd never done anything to the woman, so didn't understand Kendall's clear distaste for her.

"It's getting late, Hyde. Are we going to get any work done tonight?" Kendall asked, her tone scathing.

"Oh, my god. I'm sorry," Gypsy scrambled for

words. "I never meant to keep you. I should be getting to bed anyway, early morning and all—"

"Stop, Gypsy." Hyde stood and crossed his arms over his broad chest. "I'm not working tonight, Kendall. Call it a personal day. I may not work the rest of the week either. And that's my choice, not yours. What you did today... I don't, no, I *can't* work with you right now."

Gypsy stood as well, her brain puzzling together his words and attitude. "Wait. What did she do today?"

Hyde scoffed and extended an open hand toward Kendall. "You can thank her for your afternoon with the police."

"What?"

"Kendall reported the car stolen, which is why you were picked up."

Seeing red, Gypsy marched over, raised her hand, and slapped Kendall across the face as she hissed, "You bitch."

"Aunt G?"

Gypsy spun around to see a sleepy Tina standing in the doorway and watching everything unfold. Perfect. She shot Hyde a look that said there would be further discussion at a later time, then moved toward Tina, opening her arms.

"Hey, kiddo. Were we too loud? I'm sorry. Come on, let's get you back to bed."

"I want some water."

"Sure thing. Then back to bed."

She got the water, hugged Tina, and then led her away, trying to ignore the hushed whispers between Hyde and Kendall. Trying, but failing. Gypsy could still hear, and she might have worn a smug grin noting Hyde wasn't backing down, but handing Kendall her ass.

CHAPTER EIGHTEEN

*H*yde couldn't remember the last time he'd wanted a shot so bad. Since waking up to the sound of the door slamming, he'd had just about every emotion known to man twist his psyche, and he was spent. Unfortunately, he was also too wired to go to sleep.

Things had been going so well with Gypsy until *she'd* shown up. In fact, the more Hyde thought about it, the more he realized that was the way of it. Every single time he had started to make progress with her, Kendall materialized. He could tell Tina didn't like her, and neither did Gypsy, although neither one of them would ever be so rude as to vocalize it. On any given day, his bullshit meter would have him knocking people off his give-a-shit list for lesser offenses than the chaos she created, and yet, Kendall persisted. He didn't know why he was letting her stay.

It's business.

At what point did one let business take priority over sanity?

What the hell, he thought. *One shot isn't going to kill me.*

His hand shook as he poured; the ice-cold liquid burned his throat. Hyde looked around, expecting to be caught and chastised. Of course, no one was there. He shrugged, feeling more confident, and poured another. In the corner of his office, his laptop beckoned, a silent devil luring him to look. To see if Sami had left any more surprises out there for him to discover.

His fingers tingled as the familiar flush rode his body. Warming from his gut outward, Hyde welcomed the sensation like an old friend. In a fit of childish impetuousness, he gave his computer "the bird" and turned the light off.

He'd taken two steps out into the hall before he stopped, and went back in to finish the Effen.

What's a couple more shots anyway?

Images and snippets of various conversations with Gypsy raided his brain while Hyde's feet carried him downstairs. As he began digging out box after box of Halloween decorations and dropping them in the entryway, he could hear her sweet giggles. Satisfied he'd retrieved everything from all the places he stashed the ghastly adornments, he began opening boxes and digging through them. Her scent, clean and natural with a hint of something floral, lingered, driving him mad. Because, he had to be imagining it. Nothing was making sense other than he needed to reach Gypsy, to talk to her. To beg her to see beyond the disaster he was.

The hard knock of his fist on her door brought him back to some semblance of awareness, and Hyde managed to spare a thought for propriety before his hand closed around the knob.

Stumbling into the dark of her room, he whisper-yelled her name, but was met with silence. He called out again and took a few more steps, until his knees hit the bed.

"Gypsy?" he tried again, and then fell forward. His body sprawled across the mattress and his face hit a mound of soft, fluffy pillows that definitely smelled like her.

He smiled, then snored.

◠

A weird chime pierced at Gypsy's brain. She wasn't familiar with it, yet it wrapped skeletal fingers around her cranium and pulled. The longer it persisted, the closer to consciousness she became. It was Tina asking what she was doing in her bed that had Gypsy bolting to her feet and looking left to right in a panic.

It took several seconds and some deep breaths to remember she'd taken her niece back to bed after Kendall had interrupted her and Hyde's evening. In her effort to fend off the horrors of the day, she'd crawled in with Tina to cuddle her like she'd done when the girl was a toddler, and then she'd fallen asleep.

"I guess I crashed and never left. Sorry about yesterday, kiddo."

"S'okay. I actually had a pretty cool time with Hyde. He recorded some of this story I've been working on."

Gypsy studied the girl's smile, looking for any falsehood or hidden emotions. She saw none.

"Yeah? That's neat." After a pause, she added, "So, you're writing?"

While she loved that Hyde had stepped up in her absence, Gypsy wondered why he hadn't told her about this. They'd talked for quite a while before Kendall had interrupted – again – so, why didn't it come up? Knowing what Hyde's usual recording material was, she now worried *what* her niece was penning.

Tina's smile shifted, becoming less relaxed. "It's nothing. Just a silly kid's story about mythical creatures."

She sighed. "Wow, cool. Maybe I can read it sometime." Gypsy wasn't sure if she was offering, or asking.

"Yeah, maybe." Her fingers twisted in the hem of her tee. "So, is everything okay?"

"Hm? Oh, yesterday. Yeah, yeah. The appointment went longer than expected, and then—" she paused. Tina didn't need to know about the arrest or Kendall's deceit. "Traffic," she finished.

The expression on Tina's face said she knew Gypsy was withholding part of the story, and she almost told her about the money because of it. At the last second, Gypsy decided her niece didn't need to know about that either. Not yet anyway.

Gypsy clapped her hands and looked around. "Right. I'll get out of here and let you get ready for school. Pancakes?"

Tina grinned. "Chocolate chip?"

"You got it." Her excuse for exiting secured, Gypsy darted off to work on breakfast.

The next couple of hours passed in relative quiet. She got breakfast done, stacking the pancakes under a towel as they came off the griddle. Moving on to the clean-up, Gypsy had the kitchen back in order by the time Tina joined her. She sipped her coffee as the girl ate, and once Tina was on the bus, Gypsy took a stroll around the neighborhood. The chilly fall morning was too perfect not to enjoy before returning to the house.

Gypsy wasn't sure what had happened after she'd left Hyde and Kendall, but she'd found a literal disaster in the main hall. It looked like a Halloween store had thrown up in Hyde's entryway. Sidestepping pumpkins and witches, she headed to the sanctity of her side of the house, and her bed. As she entered her room, Gypsy pulled her shirt up and over her head while kicking the door closed behind her. After a quick rinse in the shower, she toweled off then sauntered toward her bed, ready to take a much-needed nap. The adrenaline rushes from yesterday had left her drained.

She screamed at the sight of Hyde's sleepy grin beaming back at her from her nest of pillows.

"Oh, my god. You nearly gave me a heart attack. What the hell, Hyde? What are you doing in here?"

"Slept here," he stated, and his eyes shifted over her. He was still grinning, his dimples deepening.

"What?" Even as she asked, it dawned on her that she was standing there naked. Of course, he was smiling. She yanked at the throw blanket folded over the end of the bed and wrapped herself in it.

Hyde sat up, drawing his knees toward his chest and wrapping his arms around them. "You're beautiful, Gypsy. I came to find you. To tell you I can't stop thinking about you."

"Are you drunk?" The words tumbled from her mouth before her brain had time to question them.

For half a second, she was horrified with herself, but then he laughed and said, "That's beside the point."

Her jaw dropped. She hadn't meant it, not really, when she'd suggested it. His confirmation left her feeling sorry for him, though. Things must have taken a turn for the worst last night, but that wasn't her problem. He was a big boy.

"Oh, Hyde."

The hopeful look in his sapphire-colored eyes faded.

It was time to put an end to the infatuation. This wasn't her first rodeo; she knew how to close off. Gypsy fired off the next words knowing exactly how they would land, and her gut twisted in pain.

"Go sleep it off. There's nothing for you here."

CHAPTER NINETEEN

"It itches."

Tina squirmed, and Gypsy managed to pull the pin back before stabbing her niece.

"I'm sorry, but, you need to hold still if you don't want to get jabbed." She held up the tiny weapon in her hand for emphasis.

"But—"

"No buts. I warned you, same as your mom, Halloween has never been my thing. This is all on you and Hyde. You wanted this costume for tomorrow night."

"I didn't think I'd have to be a living statue to get it."

The girl harrumphed and crossed her arms

with an adorable pout which had Gypsy looking down to avoid being caught smiling. Pure stubbornness was driving her to attempt this by hand. It would have been much easier to go to the store or order something off the internet. At least, now it would be.

Three weeks had passed since she'd become "rich," at least in her world, but she'd yet to tell anyone, rather pretending it hadn't happened. Who would she tell anyway?

She'd seen Hyde as many times in as many weeks.

In her heart, she hoped and prayed he remembered his promise to Tina. Considering he'd been hungover, possibly still drunk, the last time they'd spoken more than half a dozen words to each other, she had her reservations. Her one hope was that, although *they* hadn't spoken much, he had followed through and put the decorations up with Tina. The girl had dragged her through the house and yard multiple times over the last week to see each time they added more or made adjustments.

If he stood Tina up, then Gypsy was going to have to take her niece to this thing. A concept which revolted her.

"You could be a ghost. I'm sure I could find an old sheet around here."

"Ha. Ha."

"Hold still, then." Gypsy went back to pinning, wondering when Tina had started developing curves as she referred to the image of Bilbo Baggins one more time and tried to figure out how to make her niece's budding chest less noticeable.

She had raided Hyde's decoration stash to help out. Rough trousers from a scarecrow, a ruffled cotton shirt from an animatronic skeleton pirate, and a felt hat from a stuffed pumpkin, which Tina's dark locks would be braided and tucked up under, were among the props she'd pilfered. Per her niece, Hyde had been tasked with forging Sting.

Or is that foraging for Sting? she thought with a tiny giggle before sobering. With a sigh, her thoughts turned to what she'd do if Hyde failed. She supposed she could strip the pirate some more. There was a plastic sword thingy in its hand which would do fine.

Hyde clutched his head as the alarm blared out beside him. Kendall stirred, but didn't wake while he got up and stumbled toward the bathroom. It wasn't until he was washing his hands that the fog started clearing and he realized he was up earlier than usual, after being up extra late. They'd recorded the last chapter of *Tristan's Treasure*, and then celebrated. Hard.

He went back to check the time on his phone, and found himself staring down at his bedmate and contemplating how she'd gotten there.

After all but throwing himself at Gypsy, she'd shut him down cold. He'd tried staying sober the first few days after, even sticking to his promise of converting the house with Tina. It had, dared he admit, been the most fun he'd had doing it in years. As far as kids go, she wasn't a bad one. In all honesty, she was refreshing and he didn't mind her company; the way he didn't really mind Randy's affections either. Still, his efforts with her didn't seem to be winning him any points with Gypsy, and with reminders of her all around the downstairs, he'd taken to spending more time upstairs. By week two, his mic and a finger of vodka were always ready to go.

Kendall had smelled the rift between him and Gypsy, he knew, and had moved in like a shark to bloodied water because of it.

He didn't care.

Letting her into his bed kept him distracted when he wasn't working. And, to be honest, the chapters seemed to be getting done faster with the woman by his side. Instead of every chapter, Sami was now sending back every third or fourth one for edits. They usually involved one of the racier scenes, which he credited to Kendall's newness at narrating; she was still given to occasional fits of giggles while performing some of the lines.

It was Kendall who'd suggested—over shots, of course—that they do an "actual" run-through of a scene before they recorded it. At the time, or being more specific, given his current state of inebriety, the idea had sounded brilliant to him. A few hours later, they'd nailed it, in both the literal and figurative sense. From there, they'd fallen into a buzz-enhanced routine of drinking, fucking, and recording. Which was fine, because the less he bumped into Gypsy, the better.

Blinking away his recollections, he tried to remember why he'd set an early alarm while he freshened up. After a while, noises from downstairs drew his attention, and he went to investigate after stopping by his office to grab the gift for Tina. It was hard not to laugh at what he found.

The elven woman he'd been trying so hard to wipe from his mind was wrestling with the animated pirate he'd ordered during last year's Halloween clearance sale on Amazon.

Tonight was Tina's dance at school, and he was supposed to take her. He'd also been put in charge of the finishing touch to the girl's costume, the infamous dagger Bilbo claimed from the troll's hoard. An item which wasn't even close to the broad sword Gypsy was attempting to wrest from its glued confinement.

"It's attached," he said as he stepped forward and revealed his presence. The way her back tensed at the sound of his voice didn't surprise him, but it still cut a little. "And you don't have to steal the scabbard. I've got a dagger for Tina to use." He held out the replica he'd ordered, waiting for her to see it.

She turned around and Hyde found it hard to breathe. Her eyes never failed to stop him in his tracks when she was processing emotions. Gypsy didn't like to say much, but she didn't have to. Those eyes did all the talking for her.

"I wasn't sure. It's getting late and Tina is pacing her room."

She let her gaze fall to his hands, and he had a

moment of satisfaction when he saw the realization in them as she looked over the franchise packaging then swept upward to take in his fresh appearance.

He smiled.

"I-I'll go get her. Be right back."

Hyde watched from the sidelines as Tina made her way over to a group of kids she'd said were friends. She'd loved the dagger, and surprised them both when she launched herself at him for a hug. He was fidgety, and felt way too sober. If the lighting were better, he was sure he'd see everyone staring at him. He *was* certain he was hearing barely veiled whispers from the other chaperones about "the hermit." Murmurs of *"Is that the crazy guy?"* and *"Weren't his parents murdered in their sleep?"* reached his ears, pushing him deeper into the shadows.

The trouble with that, was it left him to his thoughts. He'd do better to go find one of the teachers to chat up or, maybe, he could go volunteer to man the punch bowl. Anything to keep him busy for the next three hours. To his dismay, a group of mother's were at the refreshment table when he approached and asked about what he could do. The way they looked him up and down as they swarmed around him, made Hyde feel like one of the snacks being offered.

He made the best of it, though. The music wasn't awful; points to him for recognizing one of the songs from the album he'd bought Tina the day they went school shopping... "High Hopes," he thought the name was. Every few minutes, his eyes scanned the gymnasium to check on Tina. Satisfied she was doing okay, he'd return his attention to whomever was in front of him. When the women asked him questions, he kept his answers polite, but brief. After a couple of hours, Hyde had to laugh at himself. Six months ago, he would have been eating their attention up, and handing out turn numbers for a go with him—a one-nighter—at one of the hotels in town.

Who was he kidding? The Hyde of six months ago wouldn't even be here. That he was, was all because a certain wanderer had come into his life and cast a spell on him.

Hyde was in the middle of pouring out a cup of punch when an eruption of laughter and noise drew his attention across the gym. A crowd had formed, and students were flocking to something unfolding on the dance floor. Gut instinct had him surveying the space, looking for Tina's felt hat. It wasn't hard to spot. She was taller than her classmates, and so it took him mere moments to see her hat rising from the center of the gathering group. Her face was a picture of mortification.

Hyde ran.

He didn't stop to think, he simply dropped the ladle and cup into the punch bowl, and ran. The closer he got, the less he had any clue what was going on. Tina kept turning in a staggered circle, her eyes darting between the ground like she wished it would open and swallow her, and looking out over the heads of her classmates. When her sight locked on him, something snapped in the girl and she burst into tears.

It surprised him enough that he stumbled and, without meaning to, pushed a few of the bystanders out of the way. He mumbled rushed apologies but hurried through the opening created. Time came to one of those dramatic, slow warped crawls while his eyes took snapshots of the scene for his brain to process. As the pieces fell into place, time sped back up to normal.

Under the sparkling disco ball, he could tell Tina's pants were wet in the back. And no matter which way she tried to turn, there were kids seeing it, and laughing. All around him, the vitriol-laced things coming from their mouths reminded him why he'd hated middle school.

Kids were fucking brutal.

Hyde scoured the crowd, searching for the punk who'd spilled punch on her. Discerning no one with an obvious expression of guilt, it dawned on him that maybe she'd had an accident. In the meantime, Tina had run to him, and now she wrapped trembling arms around his middle. He leaned over, hugging her back.

"Come on, kid. Let's get you out of here."

She nodded against his stomach, then squeezed tighter while he led her to the car.

CHAPTER TWENTY

G ypsy stood at the door, watching the Ford drive away with her niece and... *him.*

"Argh!"

She'd been losing her shit, convinced Hyde was standing Tina up so she was going to have to stand in, and had been caught off guard when he'd walked in while she fought with that damn toy. It wasn't fair he'd smelled so good, or that the clean, fresh shave he was sporting paired with a snug band tee and jeans had turned him into some kind of cover model. The devil inside her head had started whispering pleas to find a reason to go with them, so that they could keep the other women away. And, of course, so they could keep smelling him. If he weren't ten years her senior, she'd feel like a cougar.

Remembering how she'd become tongue-tied at the sight of him, and then shocked by the lengths he'd gone to for Tina, Gypsy shook her head to fend off the ludicrous notions starting to form. Hyde didn't belong to her, she had no claim on him. How many times did she have to remind herself of this? She didn't want him anyway. Hell, he'd made no secret Kendall had taken up residence in his bedroom. The two were keeping the same hours, her laundry now mixed with his, and the dirty dishes they left behind for her to do were always in sets of two. Gypsy was surprised the weasel hadn't tried to go along tonight.

On second thought, no, she wasn't. Kendall didn't do kids.

Closing the door, Gypsy made her way to the kitchen for a glass of water. It would be several hours before they got home, and she felt restless. Wired. *Horny*, she admitted to herself. She hadn't gotten off since her time with Hyde, what with Tina in the room right next to hers, and the overall stress she'd been under. Leaving the glass by the sink, she wandered out into the house and through the rooms, looking and listening for any sign of

Kendall. Going back to the front door, she opened it and scanned the yard. She didn't see any sign of the bitch's car, so assumed she had the place to herself.

Moving to the den, she turned on the television and proceeded to channel surf for the next half hour. Nothing was catching her attention so she clicked it off. Thinking a walk would help burn off whatever the nervous energy buzzing through her was, she fetched her shoes and phone, and headed out.

The sun had set by the time she got back. As she strolled down the dark driveway, and toward the dark house, she wished she'd thought to flip the porch light on before going out. Off to her right, something rustled in the trees. An image of the bobcat came back to her and while she didn't start running, she did start moving with more purpose. Reaching the porch, it dawned on Gypsy that Kendall's car was still gone. Her walk had been refreshing, but it had been quiet enough for her head to go a mile a minute the whole time. While she felt less restless now, she was still randy.

What the hell, why not?

She latched and locked the door then practically ran to her room, a sudden surge of naughtiness making her excited to get down to business. In her room, she opted to leave the door ajar so she could hear if anyone came home. Hyde and Tina weren't due back for a while, but she had no idea where the bimbo had gone, or when she'd return.

Gypsy stripped down to her bra and panties, grabbed her phone, and crawled onto her bed to settle in the nest of pillows. After a few taps on the screen, she reclined back to watch the porn she'd chosen. It didn't take long before her body began reacting, her nipples hardening as the need to squeeze her legs together grew. Trailing fingers over her chest, her breaths deepened while she started teasing herself. When the man on the screen lowered his mouth to a bared breast, she closed her fingers over a nipple, and pinched. Her moan matched the woman's in the video clip as Gypsy closed her eyes. She could still hear the noises, the sexy whispers and wet kisses, but in her mind the actors had changed. Now it was her breasts being suckled.

And Hyde was doing the suckling.

Her eyes flew open and she dropped the phone. It was then she realized she also heard voices out in the house. Bolting from the bed, she ran for the door to close it, but stopped as Tina appeared and started to knock. She barely got the door open before her niece came at her. The girl's arms wrapped around her, so Gypsy cradled her back, asking what was wrong while Tina's tears wet her midsection.

"She had a small, um, accident at the dance."

Gypsy's head shot up. Hyde was standing there holding a drug store bag and somehow ignoring she was in her underwear.

"I didn't know what you might have or what she might need, so I just grabbed a few things. Hopefully one of them works." He looked embarrassed, but also concerned as he shoved his purchases at her.

It was charming.

She reached for the bag and glanced inside. "Oh." Of course, it should've occurred to Gypsy this would happen. It was nature, after all. Hugging Tina, she asked, "Do you understand what's going on?"

Her niece nodded, and Gypsy sighed in relief. She had no idea what Gloria had shared about this "magical time in a young girl's life," but she was glad Tina at least knew the basics. They could talk later, when the inevitable questions started coming.

"Why don't you go take a warm shower, kiddo? I'll fix you some cocoa for after you get cleaned up." She dug around in the bag, pushing aside boxes of tampons in every size imaginable and industrial-sized overnight pads to choose a box of standard pads, which she handed to her niece. "I think you can figure these out, but ask if you need help."

Tina snatched the box and tucked it under her arm, trying to hide it, and with a mumbled, "Thanks," ran off.

After the girl scurried to the bathroom, Gypsy turned to Hyde. This time, he looked. It was brief, but his blue eyes dipped down before coming back to meet hers.

Hyde had been trying not to stare since the door had opened. Now that the girl wasn't standing between them, he couldn't resist. The smirk she wore when he brought his eyes back up told him he'd been caught, and he shrugged. He wasn't ashamed that he found her beautiful.

"So, sounds like it was an eventful night?"

Gypsy folded her arms over her chest, modesty taking hold, and leaned against the door.

"You could say that." He laughed. "Here's the sad part, getting to play dad to a first time period crisis wasn't the worst part of the night."

Gypsy looked at him, and smiled. "Oh?"

"Have you heard the gossip that goes on when PTA moms get together?"

Hyde managed to keep a straight face until Gypsy broke, and then they shared a deep belly laugh. When it settled, he lobbed the question back at her.

"Eventful night for you, too?" he said, pointing at her state of undress. The way she blushed, everywhere, triggered his baser desires.

"Huh, this, um…"

She was stammering and stuttering, and Hyde became positive they'd caught her being naughty. *Fuck,* he thought as his mind began filling with images.

"I went for a walk, and was getting ready to grab a shower when y'all got here—"

He heard a low moaning coming from the direction of her bed and pushed into her room, her rambling stopping the second he passed her.

"Hey, where are you going? Wait, what—"

Her words cut off a second time when he reached her bed and found her phone.

"Put. That. Down," Gypsy ordered.

Curiosity behind his grin, Hyde flipped it over to take a look. He watched the video for a few seconds, approving of her choice, before she tried grabbing it from his hand with a loud, "Oh, my god, please!"

She was now beet red and all he wanted to do was wrap her up in his arms and kiss the ever-loving shit out of her. It wasn't easy keeping his hands to himself. In particular when he held the phone up, just out of her reach. Her attempts to jump up and get it were knocking her off balance so she had to brace against him. The feel of her hand and the heat radiating from her body, along with the scents of her shampoo and sweat had his senses buzzing.

Through her obvious embarrassment, she glowed. Her eyes shone and although her chest heaved with exhilaration, there was something about her which stopped him in his tracks. Hyde became serious, stepping closer to her as he brought his hand down and handed the phone to her. As she took it, he let his arm slide around her waist and then pulled her flush. He was going to kiss her if she didn't stop him.

"Gypsy..."

Her hand came up between them, almost timid as she pressed it to his chest and pushed him back. "You're with Kendall."

She opened her mouth to say something else, but he left before she could say anything, or see the devastation he felt in his eyes.

CHAPTER TWENTY-ONE

The stone bench was cold beneath him, yet Hyde welcomed it as he sat there, elbows on his knees, head in his hands. It'd been an emotional morning, and he wanted a drink. Needed it even. Not wanting to oversleep or disappoint Tina, Hyde hadn't consumed any alcohol since his shot on Friday night. He'd spent yesterday avoiding the cravings by going on a ten-mile run, in a cold drizzle. It'd been draining, in a good way, except now he had a low-grade fever. Two weeks had zipped by since Halloween, but he still had a week until his brother and family would be infiltrating his house, which would plenty of time to get over a runner's cold. He hoped so, anyway.

When Connie first called, suggesting the Thanksgiving meal be at his place this year, he'd laughed and hung up. Zeke had called back about twenty minutes later and talked some sense into him. With Gypsy and Tina here, it would be the kind thing to do. Not to mention, Connie's due date was the first of December, so they were hoping to take some of the stress off her shoulders by "letting" *him* play host. Then, Zeke drove the final nail of guilt in by reminding Hyde it was Tina's first holiday season without her parents. While none of that should have mattered to Hyde, it did. In the last few months, two females had started mattering more to him than he ever thought anyone would, no matter how hard he tried to tamp down the feelings. And, after today, he had to admit he found himself almost looking forward to the family gathering. To him, it felt like he was being given a second chance at happiness, so long as he didn't fuck up. Some days were harder than others, but he was trying.

Kendall was another situation. He hadn't been with her since the night of the school dance, and she wasn't even close to a happy camper about it. Good thing they'd wrapped the final chapter before he asked her to move back to her room, and out of his, because if looks could kill...

"I'm sorry, what? I don't think I heard that right."

"I want you to gather your stuff from my room and go back to yours. I- I can't keep doing this... whatever this is I'm doing."

"How dare—"

He cut her off as her pitch started to rise. "I'm sorry, Kendall. I never should have let things go this far between us. It was unprofessional, and for that, I am sorry." Hyde paused to see if she was going to try to yell again. When she did nothing but stare at him and seethe, he went on, "But, yeah. I need you to go back to your space. We've sent the last chapter to Sami, now we wait for her to get back to us. Once she's signed off on them all, and we know there are no more edits to be done, I'll cut you a check. I'll expect you to be gone soon after, so you might want to start making arrangements."

It was cold and heartless, but Hyde had no choice. If he didn't start owning up to his responsibilities and giving a shit about himself, beginning with cutting the toxic from his life, he was doomed to sadness and heartache.

After delivering Tina to her aunt, he'd shuffled to his room following Gypsy's harsh, but deserving, dismissal to find Kendall still in his bed. Maybe if she'd still been asleep, he wouldn't have gone off, and things would be different now, but seeing her sitting there, watching TV and chomping on potato chips—and leaving crumbs everywhere—made him look wider. His eyes scanned the room and he realized what a disaster the space had become. Dishes piled on the nightstand, discarded shoes piled by the door, bras and panties tossed here and there; she'd overtaken his room, and turned it into a pigsty. As his gaze had swung back to her, he'd no longer seen a svelte blonde awaiting him in his bed.

No, he'd seen a lead weight who was going to drag him to the bottom of the river of life.

He'd left her to the room that night and gone to sleep in his studio. Since then, Hyde had been making an effort, again, to change. The first thing he'd done was pour out most of the booze. Cold turkey wasn't an option if he didn't want to get sick so he knew he'd still need a shot or two a day for a little bit. Next, he'd reset all his alarms to "normal," so that he was up by six and taking actual responsibility for his day with diet, exercise, and work. In his heart, he knew it was probably too late, but he wanted to prove to Gypsy he wasn't a lost cause.

After two weeks of venomous stares from Kendall, if they crossed each other's path, and icy cold politeness with Gypsy, he was questioning everything. The first woman had all but disappeared, and he couldn't be assed to care where she was spending her time or what she was doing. If she pulled a runner and Sami needed edits, well, then, they'd figure something out. He was confident enough in their recording and his editing skills that he doubted she'd find anything. And, at this point, if she did, he was willing to trash the whole project. He didn't need the fucking paycheck that bad. Gypsy, on the other hand, was around; cleaning his home, cooking his food, and mothering her niece. She always had a soft smile for him, but her eyes didn't sparkle the way he'd seen before, the way he knew they could when she was happy. In his gut, he knew that shine had dimmed because of him.

Tina seemed to be the only one he could breathe around right now. Maybe it was the bond they shared. Losing your parents as a kid changes something in a person.

"It's very peaceful here."

Her quiet voice drew him from his thoughts, and he looked up and around, his eyes landing on the marble tombstone in front of them as he bounced his knees; the cool fall air was causing incessant fidgeting. The second grave today, this one was older and nothing like the still crisp marker and barely seamed sod of Gloria's final resting place. Bits of moss had begun creeping up over the base of his parent's memorial and the marble had a weathered appearance now. An autumnal bouquet of sunflowers, mums, and goldenrod overflowed the stone vase between their names.

Miss Daisy had been at the gate, much to his relief, and though she'd tried to stand from her chair to hug him, he'd bent to her level to hug her, and then introduced her to his company. Seeing as she was the closest thing he had to a living mom, her approval meant everything. Her beaming smile and the way her dulled eyes had brightened had said what he needed to hear.

"It is. I should come more often."

"You should. I'll come with you anytime you want," Tina offered.

Hyde felt his eyes get wet. The sentiment was

simple, but heartfelt. She'd been helping him box up the Halloween decorations when an heirloom piece had prompted her to ask about his parents. He'd given her the version he hoped wouldn't give her nightmares. Keeping it simple, he'd explained they'd gone in a tragic accident at the same time, while he was away at school. When she'd then asked him when he'd last gone to see them, he'd been shell shocked by her concern, until they'd talked a little more.

One of the things Tina hadn't done in her grieving yet, was go to her own parents' graves. To be fair, she hadn't asked Gypsy to take her, so her aunt didn't know it had been weighing on the girl's mind. That afternoon, though, she confessed it to him, and then, with a, *"If you'll take me to see my folks, I'll go with you to see yours,"* Tina propositioned him.

"Deal." He'd said it then, and he agreed again now.

Tina sat down on the bench and nudged his shoulder with her own. "Why don't you introduce us?"

Gypsy's heart was breaking and rebuilding while she watched the pair. It had been a hard morning. Part of her wanted to move closer, to hear what they were saying, but she knew there was more to what was happening right now than she understood. Yes, her family was gone, *now*. Unlike Hyde and Tina, she'd enjoyed having her parents around until her twenties—and she hadn't all but lost them at the same time. She'd had time to process each death.

Earlier in the week, Hyde had approached her while Tina was at school. She'd just returned from doing the grocery shopping when he met her in the driveway, offering to help carry the bags in. It had almost been cute the way he'd tap-danced around, attempting generic conversation until she'd told him to just get to it. When he finished telling her about the talk he and Tina had, and then followed it up by asking her permission to take Tina to the graves, her first reaction had been disappointment —in herself. For yet another thing she hadn't considered where her niece's well-being was concerned.

Hyde had no idea what a lifeline he'd been for her, and Tina, since this crazy ride had started in the spring. She wanted to fall for him, and had started to on multiple occasions, but she couldn't trust such an action. Every relationship, besides the one with her sister, had always ended with her running. Why would this one be any different? Gypsy feared long term commitments, be they with other people or to a single place. She couldn't be tethered, or dependent on anyone but herself, and worried about becoming bored. If her life became stagnant, if the adventures stopped, then what was the point?

"Hey, Aunt G," Tina called, and waved.

Sitting beside her niece, Hyde wore a sad smile as he also waved. They were inviting her over. Her heart skipped a beat, but seeing the two of them watching her, hopeful expressions on their faces, they couldn't be ignored. Gypsy realized they were a pair to be reckoned with, and splitting them up might do more damage to Tina than she could fathom, and that scared her to death.

Plastering a smile on her face, she strolled toward them, one of the hardest decisions she'd ever made solidifying in her mind.

Gypsy spent the next day making preparations. In between phone calls, she flittered to and fro, most of it in the kitchen. Clearing out perishable items, she made, then packed away in the freezer, an enormous number of meals including enchiladas, lasagna, and roasted turkey breast. She even managed a chicken fried steak meal, with potatoes and gravy; this came with a hand written card instructing how to reheat the various components. Exhaustion should have taken over her with the amount of cooking and cleaning she'd done, but nervous energy kept her moving. No sooner did she go sit down, than another idea would hit her, and she'd be back in the kitchen. Kendall came through at one point, absconding with a yogurt. Even Hyde poked his head in and commented at the smells while he refilled a water bottle.

"Thought I'd make the next couple of weeks easier by getting ahead on meals," she'd chirped in response to his lip-smacking inquiry of what she was doing.

With a pecan pie and a couple batches of cookies—oatmeal cranberry and chocolate chip—cooling, she prepped one last meal for dinner that night. The ratatouille used the last of the fresh vegetables and garlic on hand.

Dinner was amicable at best, the atmosphere unsettled. While Kendall had been oddly absent of late, she'd been around today, and joined them when Gypsy used the house intercom system to announce supper. The blonde rambled on about pointless things, like how she'd gotten her car back from the collision center and how they'd said they didn't think pine cones had done the denting to the hood, but the rest of them remained stoic—other than Hyde's enthusiasm over how this was his favorite meal she fixed, which, of course, she knew.

Later that night, when the house had gone quiet, Gypsy ordered an Uber then moved the luggage she'd stashed in the coat closet by the front door earlier that day, out to the end of the drive-way. Tina was groggy and disoriented while Gypsy shook the girl awake, helped her into her coat and slippers, and then guided her up the drive to wait the few minutes left.

Guilt twisted her gut as the car carried them away.

It's for the best.

Thank you for everything, but it's time we moved on and let you go back to your life, and your normal routines. You don't need us around. It's for the best. ~G

Hyde refolded the piece of paper for the umpteenth time after staring at the scrawled words, then tucked it back into his nightstand. His hands shook, understanding eluding him. He'd replayed Sunday, and the days leading up to it, so many times in his head, trying to figure out if something had happened while they were at one of the cemeteries, or when they'd stopped for a late lunch at the local diner in Grover. Of course, it hadn't been a jovial day, but he'd been certain it was therapeutic for him and Tina. Gypsy, too. She would be the last one to admit it out loud, but she still needed to mourn her sister. The woman had fretted so much over her niece, Hyde believed she'd failed to look after her own wellbeing.

Was that why she was gone?

The three of them had gone back to his place and watched a movie before doing a simple dinner of sandwiches and carrot sticks. Saying their goodnights, he'd thought everything was good.

Clearly fucking not.

Finding her cooking all the things in the kitchen the next day should have been a red flag, but rather than read into it, he'd assumed she was processing the day before. Her offhand reply of making the holidays simpler had seemed legit to him. Now, he saw her actions for what they were. She'd been preparing to run.

From what? Me?

It confused him she'd even bothered to care, since she was leaving. That she'd left in the first place bewildered him more, and had been boggling his mind for the last two days, causing sleep to evade him.

Zeke, Connie, and the kids were due by nightfall; they were coming up once his brother got off work. He had one last chapter to revise with Kendall, and then the book "should" be finalized to Sami's specifications. She'd never been so particular on a project. After two weeks of hearing nothing from her, his email had been bombarded Monday with requests for assorted tweaks. According to her, Sami had listened to the book again, from the beginning and in one go, which is why he hadn't heard from her. In doing so, she'd found some additional issues. He'd thought he would blow off the project if more edits were requested, but he'd found Gypsy's note first, so latched onto the excuse to think about anything other than her and Tina's disappearance.

Because he didn't want to believe Gypsy was gone.

On multiple occasions Kendall had tried to cozy up to him as they handled the tweaks one by one. Each time he brushed her off, and then ignored her hot stares. More than once she tried to coax him to the freezer, to pour a shot, but each time he cut her off. If she'd bothered to open the appliance, she would've discovered there was nothing to shoot. He'd finished his limited reserve Friday night. Didn't mean there wasn't a desperate yearning to feel the icy liquid burn his throat even as his stomach clawed at him.

At five days sober, he refused to give in.

After a short, unfulfilling yoga session, because he couldn't focus and his limbs kept trembling, Hyde took a cool shower to try bringing his core temp down. Once he was dressed, he shot Kendall a text to meet him in the studio, not wanting to go searching for her. He hoped to have his commitments with her settled before his family arrived. Hyde knew the judgments were coming. It wouldn't be just Zeke and Connie wanting, no, *demanding* to know where Gypsy and Tina had gone. Aimee and Ashlee had been counting down the days to visiting their friend again, too—Zeke had made sure Hyde was well aware of this—so, when the girls weren't here, he would have some explaining to do. Problem was, how did he explain when he didn't know himself.

For the third time that day, he ran for the toilet. He was empty, nothing left to give, but his body kept trying to revolt. When he was done, he wiped his mouth and sipped on a glass of water, and then went to the studio to set up, a new film of sweat coating his skin. On the heels of everything else, Hyde's cold had turned into a bug—no doubt because he'd opened himself to all sorts of germs at the school dance—and he had every intention of heading to bed as soon they wrapped the chapter. He'd edit and send it to Sami later, even if it meant Kendall would be hanging around here a little longer. Tomorrow was Thanksgiving, so the odds that Sami would even listen to it before the weekend was over were low.

"Unca Hyde! Unca Hyde, where are you?"

Randy's unmistakable voice sang out through the house, pulling Hyde from his nap. As he sat up and rubbed the sleep from his face, he smiled. He felt like shit, everything hurt and he was burning up, but he welcomed how his heart seemed to swell at the sound of the kid's voice.

With some effort, Hyde dragged his body up from the couch and ducked into the bathroom to relieve himself and splash some water on his face. *Hello, handsome,* he thought then scoffed.

A haggard man showing every last one of his forty years stared back from the mirror. It was a good thing the chapter revisions were done, because he had to admit he wasn't doing so hot. His throat was raw and his voice was hoarse so there would be no more voice work, not until this cleared.

When he got downstairs, he found most everyone by the front door. Suitcases, coats, pillows and blankets, and shoes were strewn around the foyer, dumped unceremoniously to be moved to rooms later. Zeke and Connie, who sported a huge belly which had Hyde wondering how she wasn't toppling over, stood amongst the carnage. With Kendall.

An unnerving feeling crept over him.

The twins were elsewhere, but Randy was in awe. It was clear by the expression on his little round face that the boy was entranced as he ogled the blonde. Even if it hadn't been, Randy asking in a breathy whisper, "Are you a princess?" cemented the fact.

A loud, disbelieving laugh rumbled from Hyde, announcing his arrival and earning him a daggered glare from Kendall before she knelt down.

"Aren't you the cutest little thing," she cooed then tapped the end of his nephew's nose with a painted fingernail.

Hyde rolled his eyes. He detected the saccharin fakeness in her tone, but Randy was eating up the attention.

Randy's eyes grew as wide as his smile. "Tank you. I wike your eyes. Pwetty, wike Eester gas."

Kendall stood suddenly, whether taken aback by the boy's honesty or closeness, Hyde wasn't sure. Connie didn't give him time to think on the matter any further.

"Hyde, you look terrible. Are you sick? Why didn't you call? Who is this? Where's Gypsy?"

The questions pelted at him like icy rain and Hyde held his hand up to fend them off right as his nieces came running from deeper inside the house.

"Hey, Uncle Hyde," yelled Aimee.

"Where's Tina?" finished Ashlee.

He groaned.

"Hyde? What's up, man?" Zeke asked, and it was the breaking point.

"I'm glad y'all are here, really. Yes, I'm sick or something, so I'm going back to bed to sleep the rest of today off in hopes I've shifted it by tomorrow. Gypsy and Tina are gone. They left. I don't know more. Make yourselves at home." Hyde pivoted and began walking away, stopped, and turned back. "Oh, and that's Kendall. She's only here through next week." He made, and held, eye contact with the blonde for several pointed seconds while everyone stared at him with their mouths hanging open, then made his exit.

He was asleep within seconds of his head hitting the pillow.

CHAPTER TWENTY-THREE

Hyde swam upward toward consciousness, becoming aware of muted whispers the closer he got. Knowing he could open his eyes and be fully awake, he chose not to, hovering below the surface for a while longer. The whispers continued as he assessed how he felt: still achy, sweaty and uncomfortable, and then, the nausea hit.

He rolled from the bed and lurched toward the bathroom, catching sight of his sister-in-law and one of the twins in his peripheral when he ran by.

Connie was waiting with a glass of ice water when he came back out. "Here. Sip, don't gulp," she ordered then waddled back to the large reading chair in the corner of his room.

With a nod of thanks, Hyde took the glass. The liquid was icy cold, laced with bright lemon flavor, and delicious.

"That's great. Thank you," he croaked out.

"You're welcome." Connie went to the door and closed it before asking, "When was your last drink, Hyde?'

He held up the glass. "Uh, just now."

"You know what I mean. How many days, Hyde?"

"Five, six days. I don't know. What does it matter?" he snapped back, and Connie sighed.

"Oh, Hyde." She shuffled back to the chair and eased herself down. "Zeke and I were talking—"

"When are you not?"

Her lips drew into a tight line while she closed her eyes and drew a deep breath in.

For a guy wanting to turn over a new leaf, he wasn't trying all that hard with the people he should be. The ones who'd always shown the most concern for him. His family.

"I'm sorry," he offered, shame overtaking him.

Opening her eyes, Connie smiled. "It's Thanksgiving. I'm going to go out on a limb given your current state that you don't have anything planned. As I was saying, Zeke and I were talking, and we'd like to take you over to the country club for dinner. It's late notice so we won't get the best table, but we can get in. Zeke already called to make sure."

The idea of going out in public wasn't appealing. "I'm not feeling so good, ya know. There's a ton of food in the freezer. Gypsy went on some freak spree before she took off. We can reheat whatever looks good—"

At the look she gave him while wresting herself up from the chair, he shifted gears.

"Or, yeah, sure, country club sounds great. How long do I have to grab a shower and get dressed?"

She hesitated a heartbeat, chewing on her lip and looking around the room. It was a rare day when Constance Johnson avoided eye contact or saying what was on her mind, so Hyde braced for what was sure to be a doozy.

"We have an hour or so before we have to go. Take your time. Your, um, friend was included in the headcount. Randy insisted. She read stories to him last night, with the voices, like you do, and the boy hasn't stopped talking about her. We haven't seen her today, though, so if you could find her and invite her, for your nephew's sake, that'd be great.

Normally I'd argue and say family only, but it's just not worth the hassle. I'm tired, and today is already going to be stressful."

With that she waddled off, rubbing her lower back and leaving Hyde more bewildered than ever.

Connie insisted they take their minivan to dinner. Parking was limited and they could all agree Hyde was in no condition to drive. Kendall offered to drive the two of them in her car, but when Randy showed the first signs of an epic meltdown because he wouldn't be able to sit by her, sanity for the adults prevailed. Nobody wanted to hear the kid go off on one of his tirades. They didn't happen often, but were devastating when they did.

The vehicle bounced along under Zeke's direction, Hyde's clammy forehead resting against the cool window. Connie was doing the same up front. Beside him, Aimee and Ashlee were quiet; they'd been giving him the silent treatment. No one had said anything, but he knew they blamed him for Tina's absence. In the row ahead, Kendall looked stiff and uncomfortable while Randy chattered away beside her, explaining one toy after another as he showed her each one in his travel bag. With the short notice, she'd not had much time to get ready, so had tucked her hair up under a brown cap. Something about the look tickled a memory in his mind, but he couldn't get a grip on what. She'd seemed honestly surprised when he'd knocked on her door to ask her along, but before she could read more into it, he'd made it clear it was at Randy's request, not his. Her face had fallen. He knew she was hating this with every fiber of her being, and yet, she was trying.

Why?

Of course, the more he tried to apply reason, the less his brain wanted to cooperate.

Being upright was getting harder on him. He was hot, parched, and finding it difficult to breathe in the confines of the car. Hyde closed his eyes and let the lethargy take over for the duration of the trip.

An hour later their group was being led to a table which couldn't have been farther from the buffet, right next to the bathrooms. The twins griped, Connie and Zeke thanked the hostess seating them, and Kendall had to shift the disappointment from her face, but Hyde was grateful. While the scents of an elaborate holiday meal wafting over the dining area should have been welcoming, they were making Hyde's stomach roll.

He returned from using the facilities to find their waitress explaining what was included with the buffet and how a limited menu was also being served from the kitchen. Cutting her off by asking for water, he pushed past and helped himself to a plate of mashed potatoes and gravy from the vast spread. Ignoring Connie's disapproving look when he got back, he plopped down, put his head in his hand, and started shoveling the food in.

Hyde's focus shifted in and out as the potatoes disappeared and he sipped on water. When it no longer tasted good, he stopped eating and looked around the table. At some point, the rest had gone and filled their plates, too. No one spoke, except Randy, of course. He never stopped.

Realizing he'd rejoined the group, Connie cleared her throat. That look of uncertainty he'd seen earlier was back, and Hyde's stomached clenched, a sharp pain piercing his head.

"So, um, Hyde. After dinner, we want to take you over to Spartanburg Regional."

Clinking cutlery and murmured conversations continued on around them as sweat beaded on Hyde's skin.

"You're not sick, hon. Well, you are, but not how you think. We, Zeke and me, we think it's wonderful you haven't had a drink for a week, but we're also pretty sure you've gone into detox. And for someone who, well, who drinks as much as you, you should be under medical supervision. It's lucky you haven't had more serious complications."

Hyde stared at her, piecing the words together in his head that she'd said, not wanting to hear them, but unable to deny them.

"Fuck! Oh, my god. Ouch!" Kendall started shrieking and rubbing at her eyes. A clump of cranberry sauce dripped off her cheek onto the bodice of her light green dress.

Randy burst into tears as he dropped his spoon. "I sowwy. I was trying to share wid you," he sobbed.

Connie was scolding Kendall for her language, when the blonde went off at everyone.

"You are all insane. That brat just ruined a three-hundred dollar dress and you want to yell at me for my language?" she screeched.

Hyde was having trouble moving beyond the fact they'd lured him out with every intent to check him into rehab. When his nephew's blubbering transformed into a soft, "How you change like that?" he glanced over. Even with his own disorganized thoughts, the shift in the boy caught his attention and he looked up.

Everyone was staring at Kendall.

"What?" she asked. "What the hell is wrong with all of you?"

"Why are your eyes different colors?" Ashlee asked, speaking for the first time Hyde had heard since finding Gypsy's niece gone.

"What the actual fuck?"

"Hyde," Connie hissed, followed by her own, "Oh, fuck."

Zeke's eyes snapped to his wife as a comedy of errors seemed to unfold before Hyde.

"Connie, honey, what's wrong?"

"Mom?" Aimee and Ashlee chirped together.

His eyes traveled the table, landing on each occupant, until he got back to Kendall, who he found staring back at him, pleading, from dichromatic eyes. As he honed in on the unfamiliar brown one, so dark compared to the vibrant green he'd grown used to, then her silly brown hat, light dawned.

No fucking way. But, how?

"I think we need to get to the hospital," Connie

panted out at the same time Hyde spoke up. She was pushing her chair back.

"Sami?"

Kendall's eyes bulged, Zeke let out his own expletive, and the kids all jumped out of their seats.

"Unfuckingbelievable." Hyde threw his napkin on the table and marched out of the restaurant.

As his feet hit the pavement, the first snowflakes of the year drifted down toward the sidewalk. He hadn't gone three feet when darkness descended and he joined them.

CHAPTER TWENTY-FOUR

The lyrics coming from the radio seemed to mock her, spot on with their "two wrongs don't make a right" message, twisting the knots in Gypsy's stomach tighter. A little over four months had passed since they'd spoken. When she'd last seen him, in the hospital the day after Thanksgiving, Hyde hadn't been conscious. Her better judgment told her not to do this, to make her exit before Zeke brought his brother home. With time, and absence, she'd almost forgotten what it was like to be near him. Did she want to pick that scab off?

Never had a "break up" been so hard, and they'd never even been an official thing.

Truth be told, she was scared of her own reaction. Gypsy didn't trust she wouldn't fall right back under his spell; and she wasn't so sure it would be an awful thing if she did. At the same time, she didn't know why she was entertaining these thoughts. *She* walked out on him. He had every right to hate her. For that reason alone, and assuming today's meeting was him satisfying some step program checklist, she'd accept his claim of forgiveness, to make things easy, then leave. And, that would be that.

Worried about the day's outcome, Gypsy had packed hers and Tina's bags, again, last night. Once they had this conversation he'd requested with her, she would ask Connie to take them back to the extended stay place. The one Zeke had found her at on Thanksgiving evening...

Gypsy's phone rang for the third time in a row, finally prompting her niece to speak. Something she'd not done much of since Gypsy had stolen Tina away in the night and brought her to this hotel. She planned to call a realtor after the holiday and see if there was anything in the area affordable. Plan B would be getting them into an apartment until the end of the school year at least, until she could figure something else out.

"Oh, for crying out loud." Tina jumped up and snatched the phone from the coffee table. "Hello?"

Already up from the table and moving toward the girl, it was no more than an arm's length for Tina to pass the phone over.

"It's Zeke."

She froze. Was he calling because they'd bailed? Or, had something happened?

"Aunt G?"

Gypsy shook her head, and reached for the phone. Her hand trembled as she brought it to her ear and choked on her greeting, "Hel– hello?"

"Gypsy? Hey, I'm sorry to call you out of the blue like this. Listen, I don't know what happened, and it doesn't matter, but I need your help now."

"What's wrong?"

"I'm at the hospital with Connie, she's in labor."

"Oh, that's... wow." While happy for the couple, she didn't know why this was her concern.

"Yeah, crazy, right? We thought she had another week. But tonight got a little, uh, exciting. Connie told Hyde at dinner that we think he should check into rehab..."

Gypsy's mind wandered, not hearing the next few things. Why would Hyde need rehab? Yeah, sure, he got carried away sometimes, but he'd been so much better. Hadn't he?

Oh, shit. Had her running driven him back into the bottle? Surely not. He had Kendall. She doubted the pair of them had even noticed the lack of Gypsy and Tina's company after they'd gone.

"Gypsy? Are you there?"

"Yeah, yeah. Sorry. Got distracted for a second. What were you saying?"

"Hyde collapsed outside the restaurant, Gypsy. He took the same ambulance to Spartanburg Regional as Connie. I'm up in Labor and Delivery, they've taken my brother to the ER to stabilize him. The kids are being watched by a nurse, but they can't do that all night. I need help."

Zeke sounded so broken, so lost. In all her communication with him, Zeke was always upbeat, and above all, calm. Whatever calm he was maintaining on the surface was about to crack. She could hear it down the phone.

"What about Kendall?" Her tone was cold, but Gypsy couldn't go back to where she was second fiddle. She couldn't bear seeing Hyde with another woman anymore.

"There's a story there, but the long and short of it is, she's gone. For good."

"I have to turn off dinner to make sure nothing burns while we're gone, but then I'll call an Uber and meet you at the hospital."

"Oh, god. Thank you, Gypsy." *A single sob punctuated his barely veiled desperation.*

After that night, Gypsy and her niece had returned to the old schoolhouse, Hyde's home. Tina in tow, she'd met up with Zeke in the Labor and Delivery lounge to collect the girls and Randy, and the keys to the minivan at Zeke's insistence. Along with the keys, he crammed a bunch of bills into her hand and told her to pick up whatever they could find open on the way home. She nodded to appease him, but knowing the amount of food she'd left behind, she made straight for the house.

An hour and a half later, the den had been transformed into the ultimate blanket fort and the smell of cookies wafted through the house. Gypsy had made the call that "real" food could be eaten the next day. The kids had been through an emotional evening, and needed the escape as much as she did.

A sharp wail drew Gypsy from her thoughts. She turned to see Connie coming into the kitchen, Robby squawking in her arms.

"Here, let me," she offered, going to take the chunky boy from his momma.

Hyde's discharge happened to coincide with the kids' spring break, so they'd all come up for the week. It'd been nice having them around. Tina, in particular, had been having a wonderful time with Aimee and Ashlee. Randy had become Gypsy's baking buddy, since the girls were all too busy with nail polish, repeated viewings of the *Pitch Perfect* movies, and other general teenage girl things to give him the time of day.

As Gypsy bounced Robby on her hip and started playing Peek-A-Boo, Connie prepped a bottle.

"Thanks for sticking around today, Gypsy. It means a lot."

Over the past months their friendship had grown. While no one would ever replace Gloria, Connie was now the closest thing she had to a sister figure and friend. Especially considering some of the wars she'd had of late with Tina. Having Connie to call on for help had spared her mental state more than once. In return, Gypsy had made Connie her confidant. Next to Hyde, she knew more about Gypsy's past than anyone, but unlike Hyde, she also knew about the inheritance money. In fact, the realtor she was scheduled to meet with after the holidays was a friend of Connie's.

"It's the least I can do. Y'all have been so generous with us."

Zeke had shown her how to set up an online bank account after the chaos of Thanksgiving died down. Minor complications with the delivery kept Connie and Robby at the hospital for about two weeks. During that time, Gypsy held down the fort at Hyde's house with the kids. Via the online account, her paycheck was deposited. Zeke had doubled what Hyde was paying, insisting her work load had "at least" doubled in the madness.

Connie laughed. "No, I think... how should I say this? The universe works in mysterious ways, we all know this. In my opinion, we were all put in each other's paths for one reason or another. You've helped us, my family, as much as we've helped you and Tina." A quick test of the formula on her wrist, and she reclaimed her baby. "As I said, it means a lot that you're here. I know Hyde appreciates it, too."

There it was. Mention of the elephant in the room. Hyde had asked on a handful of occasions, through Zeke and Connie, that she come see him during the rehab center's visitation days. She hadn't been able to bring herself to do it. She didn't want to see him broken, and the thought that he was reaching out now to satisfy some to-do list, broke her. Even in his fucked up state, he'd been the kindest thing to ever happen to her. No man, not even her work-distanced father, had ever managed to make Gypsy feel appreciated the way Hyde did.

Until he didn't.

Out in the house, Gypsy heard their arrival, and her stomach dropped.

Connie smiled, gave her a quick one-armed hug, and headed out to meet them. "Take a minute, but don't linger too long. I promise, it's not as bad as you think."

So much had changed since the holiday season. Hyde had faced some of the hardest truths of his life, and overcoming them had not been easy. It was something he was still working on, and probably would be for a while. His counselor had warned him about moving too fast with Gypsy, pushing too hard. New to sobriety as he was, Cash didn't think Hyde should be jumping into a relationship.

But he hadn't met Gypsy.

She was his match, and if she didn't want him, he doubted another woman would ever do. Hyde wasn't looking for sexual satisfaction or a quick fuck. He wanted *her*. Her mind. Her heart. And he was willing to go as slow as *she* wanted, so long as she was with him.

A hush fell over the den, the exceptions being Robby's exuberant suckling and Randy's neverending chatter—he was currently on about some bugs he'd seen while playing out in the yard earlier—and without looking, he knew she was there. He could feel her proximity, sense her with every fiber of his being. All Hyde had to do was turn around to see her.

Fear of seeing rejection, or worse, in her eyes locked his movements. His heart was tender and new to all of these feelings, and Hyde wasn't sure how he would cope if it became clear she hated him.

In an attempt at working up the nerve to rotate

his body and face her, Hyde let his eyes move across the occupants of the room while he slowly pivoted. When he reached Tina, who had smiled and run to him for a hug when he'd first arrived, she was watching him. A nod and an encouraging smile gave him hope, and he went for it, spinning around.

The air whooshed out of him.

Gypsy was so much more beautiful than he'd allowed himself to remember. She was thinner, and a tad gaunt through her face, though. Telling signs of the stress she'd been under.

Because of him.

"Hi." She waved and a flash of a smile surfaced before her expression became hesitant, almost guarded.

"Hey. You look good." Could he sound more like a dork?

Her cheeks flooded with color at the compliment, and he sighed, the dread easing from his shoulders with the exhale. Behind him, his family resumed their conversations even as he blocked out the white noise and took a step forward. At his action, Gypsy's chest rose with the hitch of her breath so he paused, not wanting to rush her. For a moment, her eyelids fluttered shut, but then they opened, and the unusual lilac gray of her irises was vibrant. Although not a hundred percent certain, he was pretty sure he recognized the change as a sign of her inner resolve. Where they went from here would be determined by whatever she did next.

"You too." She shuffled a foot, and he found the unfamiliar shyness adorable. "So, how have you been?"

Hyde was able to give her a genuine smile as he answered, "Good. Better than I've been in years, to be honest. For the most part." What he wasn't telling her was how he needed at least her forgiveness before he would ever be whole.

"That's good."

"How about you? Zeke said you've been a godsend with the kids. Any chance that means you'll be sticking around?"

Gypsy's eyes showed her discomfort and he berated himself.

"Sorry, I didn't mean—"

"No, no. It's fine..." she cut him off, letting her words hang in the silence enveloping the room.

The awkwardness between them was killing him. They knew each other, had even started to build something until Sami's crazy ass ruined everything. He felt the anger ramping up and closed his eyes before taking a couple of deep breaths, a calming technique he'd been working on with Cash.

"No, it's not fine, Gypsy. I *am* sorry. For so many things. I've been working on making amends—"

"Is that what this is?" she snapped. "A box to be checked off so you can clear your conscience and move on to the next task?"

The accusation thrown at him had his head spinning. Never in a million years was his intention to say a fake apology and move on. That she could think him so heartless actually made him mad. She wasn't being fair.

Marching forward, her eyes widened as he closed in on her saying, "Jesus Christ, Gypsy. Will you shut up?" he growled and crushed his mouth to hers, his lips found hers tensing at first, then softening and parting, letting him in.

This was home. In her warmth was where he belonged, and where he wanted to spend the rest of his life. He'd never felt more conviction.

Their kiss deepened, her need for him coming through the rawness of clutching hands pulling and pushing at him. He returned it. Embracing her small frame, he cradled her to his hard chest and continued to explore her mouth. When she began to shake and he tasted salt on her lips, his world nearly shattered. She wasn't supposed to be crying.

"What's wrong?"

"Not a thing." She smiled.

"But you're crying..."

"So are you."

"No, I'm not." He reached up to find his cheeks wet, and her smile grew with his astonishment, making his heart swell and his chest hurt. "Okay, so maybe I am."

Her laugh was light and airy, and warmed him inside.

"You're a mess, Hyde Johnson, but so am I. I've missed you. I won't lie, that scares me. I'm afraid. I'm afraid to let you in, but I'm even more afraid of losing you. Of never watching you work, or hearing you laugh, or—"

Hyde closed the distance, capturing her lips yet again, and this time, she didn't resist for even a second. She molded into his arms, against his body, and it was perfect.

"You, Gypsy, are what I've been looking for all my life without even knowing it. There's still a lot of uncertainty in my life. I'm a work in progress, one that needs to get his shit together for my career, for me, and if you'll have me, for you. And Tina, of course."

Slipping from his grip, Gypsy moved to the sink and got a glass of water. He wanted to know what she was thinking, but didn't press.

"You're that sure you want us, huh? We're kind of crazy hot messes, too. I can't promise it'll be easy putting up with us." Her tone had become playful, and Hyde bit.

"Sounds like a challenge I can't wait to take on."

A squeal behind them made Hyde jump and Gypsy laugh. He turned them around to find Tina standing in the doorway watching them, the biggest smile he'd ever seen stretching the girl's face.

"Does this mean this is our home now?"

Gypsy turned her faerie eyes up to him, a silent assent for him to confirm or deny her niece's question.

"There's nothing I want more." Finding Gypsy's lips once more, Hyde's world righted itself as Tina's small arms wrapped around both of them and squeezed. Whatever was to come, he knew he could face it with these two by his side.

"'She has lovely breasts,' Dakota whispered in my ear while his hands skimmed upward, lifting my nightshirt and revealing my firm, small breasts. 'But they don't compare to yours, Lena.'"

Hyde's hands replicated the actions he spoke into the mic, sending spikes of desire through Gypsy's body and making it hard to concentrate on the script in front of her. *No Reservations* was the eighth book she'd worked on with him, but the first one where they had Hush Studios all to themselves. Zeke, Connie, and the gang had come up over the weekend for a quick visit and to pick up Tina for the summer. She and Hyde had been making use of the solitude since they'd left to christen damn near the whole house. Even as his caress awakened her body, she cringed against the ache between her thighs.

"Hey, now." She laughed. "You need to behave. We have a deadline and I need some recovery time."

"I didn't know women were aware that existed," he proclaimed with false shock as the mirth in his eyes brought forth her chuckles when he reached for her breasts again.

"Seriously, Hyde. Work first, play later." She tried really hard to keep a straight face while she admonished him, but couldn't, and amid giggles found herself being lifted and carried to the couch.

"I can't help myself. It's just so hot watching you work. I love the team we make." Kisses landed on each of her eyes and then her nose. Lifting her chin, she accepted the next one on her lips. Slow and tender, it heated her from the inside out until she began pawing at his shirt.

One little hour wouldn't mess up their deadline.

"Marry me?"

Gypsy rolled her eyes. "How many times are you going to ask me that?

"Until you say yes." He grinned and wiggled his eyebrows.

"Is it not enough that I'm your business partner and I live here?"

Hyde shook his head. "Nope."

His weight on her heavy but comfortable, she studied him.

Her independent streak was as strong as ever, so when Hyde's reputation took a slight nosedive because of his unannounced hiatus, she offered aid in the form of partner. Missed deadlines and his failure to return correspondence due to lack of outside contact while in rehab had caused his business to suffer. Something told her Gloria would approve of using the inheritance money to establish roots and invest in a future. Hyde had balked at first, of course, but when she made it clear that she didn't want to be a silent partner, that she wanted him to teach her about the business and shape her into a narrator, too, he'd changed his tune. Together, they were becoming known as a reliable team to hire and with each project they released, Hush Studios moved back up in the rankings. Business was growing despite the dark smear Sami Jackson had tried creating.

Sami, or Kendall as Gypsy knew her, had not gone quietly into the night. She had slithered off like the snake she was, but while Hyde put her out of his mind as he focused on rehab and therapy, she'd contacted lawyers. She'd bided her time, much to her own demise. The court case she tried to build claimed Hyde had shared copyrighted material, because Gypsy had seen some of the book without being an employee. Thing was, by the time she came at them, Gypsy had become half owner. The judge had thrown out the case, causing Sami to have a break down in the courtroom, thus displaying her true colors.

The last time Gypsy had seen the woman she was being escorted from the courtroom by a bailiff, a banging gavel and declarations of "contempt" shouted over the ruckus she was making. Although it shouldn't, the memory made her smile. In the end, it was Sami's reputation smeared beyond repair. Word travelled fast in the Indie book world, and once her deranged actions became known, no narrator or publisher would work with her.

"Hey."

She came back to the moment, looking into Hyde's gorgeous blues. "Hmm?"

"What's swirling around in that beautiful brain of yours?"

What *was* swirling around in her brain? That was the million-dollar question. More specific, what was swirling around in her heart? Gypsy knew one thing. For the first time in her life she was truly satiated. That itch to move, to travel and see different things, to carry her from one town to another and avoid commitments, had calmed. She was content. Happy.

"Yes."

Confusion marred his brow for a long moment before realization appeared to dawn. "Yes?" he quipped, an edge of excitement barely contained straining his tone.

"Gypsy Johnson... I like the sound of that."

"So do I, more than you know."

With everything she could want at her fingertips, she welcomed Hyde in, and her soul soared free.

THE END

(Substance Abuse and Mental Health Administration in the US. If you are outside of the US, please check your local services.)

ACKNOWLEDGMENTS

It's been a few years since I was able to type "The End" on a full length novel, and I have to throw out my love for those who helped me get here.

Again. Special thanks to my beta team: Patsi, Erin, Rae, Lisa, and Jude.

All my gratitude to Mich Feeney of Proofreading by Mich for her invaluable guidance in polishing this little tale of mine.

And not to be forgotten, my bestie and graphics extraordinaire, Tammy.

Thank you all. I hope the general reader
population enjoys Wanted as much as y'all.

Domestic engineer. Author. Burgeoning editor. And quite possibly certifiable. Believing every story can shine bright with a bit of tenacious tough love, R.E. Hargrave is thorough and to the point.

An international bestselling author, she takes storytelling and manuscript polishing seriously, working with her authors and on her own creations to ensure they come to life, crawling from the pages and into the reader's souls.

Hargrave lives on the outskirts of Dallas, TX and is married to her high school sweetheart; together they are raising three children. A native 'mutt,' she has lived in New Hampshire, Pennsylvania, South Carolina, Alabama, Texas, and California. She is fond of setting her stories—which range from the sweet to the paranormal, to the erotic and horrific— on location in South Carolina and Texas.

www.rehargrave.com
@REHargrave

OTHER WORKS BY THIS AUTHOR

To Serve is Divine, Book 1 of The Divine Trilogy
A Divine Life, Book 2 of The Divine Trilogy
Surreal, Book 3 of The Divine Trilogy

Also available in Audio

The Complete Divine Trilogy
(Special edition with bonus material)

Sugar & Spice, a novella
Haunted Raine, a novella
Unchained Melody, a novella
The Food Critic, an erotic novella
Fire Lust, an erotic novella
Slots, a graphic horror novella

Brooklyn Blues, an erotic #StripedStockingStory
novella
Ribbons & Os, an erotic #StripedStockingStory
novella
Beyond 50 (free sampler of BDSM stories)
Kah Key Honeymoon, an erotic novella under
alternate penname Ima Synner

most titles are also available in audio